Also by Nadine Gordimer

NOVELS

The Lying Days
A World of Strangers
Occasion for Loving
The Late Bourgeois World
A Guest of Honor
The Conservationist
Burger's Daughter
July's People
A Sport of Nature
My Son's Story
None to Accompany Me
The House Gun
The Pickup

STORIES

The Soft Voice of the Serpent
Six Feet of the Country
Friday's Footprint
Not for Publication
Livingstone's Companions
A Soldier's Embrace
Selected Stories
Something Out There
Jump and Other Stories

ESSAYS

The Black Interpreters
The Essential Gesture—Writing, Politics and Places
(edited by Stephen Clingman)
Writing and Being
Living in Hope and History: Notes from Our Century
On the Mines (with David Goldblatt)
Lifetimes Under Apartheid (with David Goldblatt)

Loot and other stories

Loot and other stories

NADINE GORDIMER

FARRAR, STRAUS AND GIROUX / NEW YORK

Farrar, Straus and Giroux
19 Union Square West, New York 10003

Copyright © 2003 by Felix Licensing, B.V.
Printed in the United States of America
First edition, 2003

Lines from "On Woman" and "Under Ben Bulben" by W. B. Yeats reprinted with the permission of Scribner, an imprint of Simon & Schuster Adult Publishing Group, from The Collected Work of W.B. Yeats, Volume 1: The Poems, Revised, *edited by Richard J. Finneran (New York: Scribner, 1997). Copyright 1940 by Georgie Yeats; copyright renewed © 1968 by Bertha Georgie Yeats, Michael Butler Yeats, and Anne Yeats.*

Library of Congress Cataloging-in-Publication Data
Gordimer, Nadine.
  Loot and other stories / Nadine Gordimer.— 1st ed.
    p. cm.
    Contents: Loot—Mission statement—Visiting George—The generation gap—L,U,C,I,E.—Look-alikes—The diamond mine—Homage—An emissary—Karma.
    ISBN 0-374-19090-9 (alk. paper)
    1. South Africa—Social life and customs—Fiction.   I. Title.

PR9369.3.G6 L66 2003
823'.914—dc21

                                                      2002042601

Designed by Abby Kagan

www.fsgbooks.com

1 3 5 7 9 10 8 6 4 2

REINHOLD

12th March 1908–18th October 2001

1st March 1953–18th October 2001

Contents

LOOT

Once upon our time, there was an earthquake: but this one is the most powerful ever recorded since the invention of the Richter scale made it possible for us to measure apocalyptic warnings.

It tipped a continental shelf. These tremblings often cause floods; this colossus did the reverse, drew back the ocean as a vast breath taken. The most secret level of our world lay revealed: the sea-bedded—wrecked ships, facades of houses, ballroom candelabra, toilet bowl, pirate chest, TV screen, mail-coach, aircraft fuselage, cannon, marble torso, Kalashnikov, metal carapace of a tourist bus-load, baptismal font, automatic dishwasher, computer, swords sheathed in barnacles, coins turned to stone. The astounded gaze raced among these things; the population who had fled from their toppling houses to the maritime hills ran down. Where terrestrial crash and bellow had terrified them, there was naked silence. The saliva of the sea glistened upon these objects; it is given that time does not, never did, exist down here where the materiality of the past and the present as they lie has no chronological order, all is one, all is nothing—or all is possessible at once.

People rushed to take; take, take. This was—when, anytime, sometime—valuable, that might be useful, what was this, well someone will know, that must have belonged to the rich, it's mine now, if you don't grab what's over there someone else will, feet slipped and slithered on seaweed and sank in soggy sand, gasping sea-plants gaped at them, no-one remarked there were no fish, the living inhabitants of this unearth had been swept up and away with the water. The ordinary opportunity of looting shops which was routine to people during the political uprisings was no comparison. Orgiastic joy gave men, women and their children strength to heave out of the slime and sand what they did not know they wanted, quickened their staggering gait as they ranged, and this was more than profiting by happenstance, it was robbing the power of nature before which they had fled helpless. Take, take; while grabbing they were able to forget the wreck of their houses and the loss of time-bound possessions there. They had tattered the silence with their shouts to one another and under these cries like the cries of the absent seagulls they did not hear a distant approach of sound rising as a great wind does. And then the sea came back, engulfed them to add to its treasury.

That is what is known; in television coverage that really had nothing to show but the pewter skin of the depths, in radio interviews with those few infirm, timid or prudent who had not come down from the hills, and in newspaper accounts of bodies that for some reason the sea rejected, washed up down the coast somewhere.

But the writer knows something no-one else knows; the sea-change of the imagination.

Now listen, there's a man who has wanted a certain object (what) all his life. He has a lot of—things—some of which his eye falls upon often, so he must be fond of, some of which he doesn't notice, deliberately, that he probably shouldn't have acquired but cannot cast off, there's an art nouveau lamp he reads by, and above his bed-head a Japanese print, a Hokusai, 'The Great Wave', he doesn't really collect oriental stuff, although if it had been on the wall facing him it might have been more than part of the furnishings, it's been out of sight behind his head for years. All these—things—but not the one.

He's a retired man, long divorced, chosen an old but well-appointed villa in the maritime hills as the site from which to turn his back on the assault of the city. A woman from the village cooks and cleans and doesn't bother him with any other communication. It is a life blessedly freed of excitement, he's had enough of that kind of disturbance, pleasurable or not, but the sight from his lookout of what could never have happened, never ever have been vouchsafed, is a kind of command. He is one of those who are racing out over the glistening sea-bed, the past—detritus=treasure, one and the same—stripped bare.

Like all the other looters with whom he doesn't mix, has nothing in common, he races from object to object, turning over the shards of painted china, the sculptures created by destruction, abandonment and rust, the brine-vintaged wine casks, a plunged racing motorcycle, a dentist's chair, his stride landing on disintegrated human ribs and metatarsals he does not identify. But unlike the others, he takes nothing—until: there, ornate with tresses of orange-brown seaweed, stuck fast with nacreous shells and crenellations of red coral, is *the* object. (A mirror?) It's as if the impossible is true; he knew that was where it was, beneath the sea, that's why he didn't know what it was, could never find it before. It could be revealed only by something that had never happened, the greatest paroxysm of our earth ever measured on the Richter scale.

He takes it up, the object, the mirror, the sand pours off it, the water that was the only bright glance left to it streams from it, he is taking it back with him, taking possession at last.

And the great wave comes from behind his bed-head and takes him.

His name well-known in the former regime circles in the capital is not among the survivors. Along with him among the skeletons of the latest victims, with the ancient pirates and fishermen, there are those dropped from planes during the dictatorship so that with the accomplice of the sea they would never be found. Who recognized them, that day, where they lie?

No carnation or rose floats.

Full fathom five.

MISSION STATEMENT

There was a great deal of entertaining up at the Manager's house, weekends. On Monday morning a member of the kitchen and ground staff whose job it was set off to walk fifty miles to town with the master's note for the liquor store. A case of Scotch whisky. The man walked back with twelve bottles in the case on his head, arriving on Friday. Every Friday. The feat was a famous dinner-party story, each weekend: that's my man—what heads they have, eh, thick as a log!

Roberta Blayne née Cartwright works for an international aid agency, has been based both at headquarters in New York and Geneva, and posted abroad a number of times. Her first appointment to Africa came when she was nearly forty-six and felt she looked it; she had been married once, long ago it seemed to her. The journalist husband had fallen in love with a Chinese girl while on assignment in Beijing; the marriage was an intermittent one, so to speak, each of the pair generally somewhere else and it fell into desuetude amicably. He did not share her need to have some part in changing the world, which grew in inverse proportion to any other emotional need. There were no children as a reminder of the marriage; only the tragic-eyed swollen-bellied ones of the horde waiting, here, there, for succour through the bureaucratic processes she served. Not always, or often, the direct means of putting food in their gaped nestling-mouths, but projects of policy, infrastructure, communications, trade treaties, education, land distribution by which development aid was meant to satisfy all hungers.

Could have been India. Even the European countries brought to Third World conditions by civil wars. But it was Africa; a tour of duty, a territory in the process of transformation as in most others on the African continent. She unpacked at the type of house in the capital her aid agency hired for whatever personnel in middle-level position merited. The suburb must have dated from colonial times; verandah round three sides darkening rooms with fireplaces whose chimneys were now blocked by electric heaters, a garden where loquat and bougainvillaea, gnarled as old oak, tangled above stony red earth. The bedroom she chose— there were three—was obviously the best one, this confirmed by the aura of recent occupation by her predecessor and his or her bedmate, the hangers on the rods bearing the ghosts of clothes. Her own took their place; her papers and books spread where others had been cleared away. She was accustomed to this kind of takeover. Whatever lingering presence of others was quickly erased by hers. This was a confidence acquired by the nature of international work, routine as computer competency: you have to be in constant touch with headquarters, home base in New York or Geneva, and you occupy, where others were before you and will come after, designated quarters—even though the black man who insists on waking you with tea every morning and polishes the floors, and the other who squats to tend weeds that have taken the place of flower-beds, enact old colonial rituals of a home.

Her title was Assistant to the Administrator of the programmes for this country planned by experts in New York and Geneva according to their Mission Statement. Much of the application consisted of informing New York/Geneva tactfully as possible that the Agency's plan for the country to enter globalisation couldn't be achieved quite as visualised, and concealing how she and the Administrator were deviously, prudently finding out how to go about the process—not on their own well-trained theoretical model, but in the ways the Government itself best understood how the country might practise reforms and innovations according to the circumstances in which their constituents lived, often unimaginable in New York/Geneva, and the expectations, demands, prejudices, political rivalries within which Ministers thrashed about to keep their cabinet seats. This meant not only travel into the bush and up rivers to communities where the development plan saw the local school as being thrust into the new one world with information technology equipment—and where the Administrator and his Assistant found there was no electricity in the village—but also required attentive socialising with Ministers and their various Deputies, advisors, often unidentified figures attendant and clearly influential, who would pick up in mid-sentence some wandering statement by a Minister, clarifying it briskly. Who were these men—even a woman or two? How to approach them for inside facts, for warnings or encouragements about whom to seek out to breach a Minister's generalisations, that slam of doors on undesirable realities.

She enjoyed field trips: she distrusted abstraction. —Then you're working for the wrong outfit.— Her Administrator, a Canadian, taunted her; but they got on well, he had his wife and teenage son with him, the boy enrolled at a local school as evidence of the Administrator's commitment to sharing the life of the local people wherever posted. As the bachelor woman (his wife dubbed her with mock envy), she was invited to drop in and share meals at their house where the same kind of resident tea-provider and floor-polisher had become a mate of the schoolboy, teaching him to play the guitar the traditional African way, and in turn being taught the latest pop music. In addition to the official gatherings and embassy parties, the Administrator's house was where Government Ministers and officials, members of parliament, the capital's dignitaries, judges, lawyers, businessmen, were entertained for what could be gleaned of use to the Agency's mandate. Few brought their wives along; the female Minister of Welfare and two MPs were usually the only black women present, and they were strident in their interruptions of male discourse, as they had to be to distinguish them from the wives left at home. Roberta Blayne, the Administrator and his wife, Flora, had no particular sense of being white, in this company; all three had lived with black, yellow, all races in the course of their work around the world and accepted their own physical characteristic like that between eyes with or without the epithelioid fold, noses high-bridged or flat. They were also aware that they were not always accepted by the same token among all the eminent blacks present—it's easier for the former masters to put aside the masks that hid their humanity than for the former slaves to recognise the faces underneath. Or to trust that this is not a new mask these are wearing.

For the first few months neither Ministers nor their satellites addressed Roberta Blayne beyond the usual general greeting, which then began at least to include her name—not a difficult one to recall: somebody's assistant, home-grown or imported, a genus there to be ignored. But as her Administrator, Mr Alan D. Henderson, often spoke in the plural 'we' and turned to her for her interpretation of points in an interview or observations on a field trip, the dignitaries began to recognize her as, if not one of the company of Minister of Welfare and MPs—her manner was not strident—part of a delegation, another honorary man. Her status was marked by observation that she drank whisky with the Ministers instead of the beer that was the expected choice of any entourage. A dinner-table companion might turn to her sometimes with the usual questions of obligatory interest—where did she come from?—English, of course?—what does she think of our country?—ever been in Africa—first time? —First time. India, Bangladesh, Afghanistan—but not here.— —You see you are welcome, we Africans are friendly people, don't you find.— There was a lawyer who was witty and forthright, making her Administrator and her laugh at themselves, with his anecdotes and mimicry of encounters with officials from aid agencies. —One thing you development fundis don't know about is the new kind of joke you've inspired among us in the taverns.— The Administrator was equal to the banter. —It's a good sign when you hear you're the butt of humour, means you're accepted.—

The lawyer, with lips everted expectantly in a grin, saw the Assistant was about to speak: —As what? Part of the community? Or part of the scene playing between donor and beneficiary?—

—Ah, she's right on, man!— The lawyer flung himself back in his chair delightedly. —Is it a sitcom, miniseries starring the IMF and World Bank—

The Administrator was enjoying himself. —Oh not your standard villains—

This sort of pleasant exchange struck up only after the tap on a glass signalled that the host, Minister or Chairman, was about to make a welcoming speech, and discussion of the latest announcements or 'pending' announcements (development topics had their own evasive lingua franca) on trade tariffs, bills coming before parliament for land reform, proceedings of Mercasur, SADEC, the EU, had been respectfully listened to or contested (the listeners asserting themselves to become the listened to) over the skill of eating and drinking without appearing to be aware of this lowly function.

It was only then that whatever everyone had been drinking released the individual from the official; the volume rose convivially. The Administrator's Assistant felt a hand on her arm or met an assessing smile—not at all bad, this aid agency woman, the flush on the flesh where breasts lift it above her dress.

But there were not many such moments, she wasn't bothered by men; and that was perhaps not flattering. Earlier assignments, other parts of the world, it had been rather different. The attitude she had learned to convey to keep undesirables at bay without offending (aid agency work implied diplomacy above all, personal feelings must be discounted in the philosophy of equal partnership between donor agency and the people of a recipient country): that defence was scarcely needed, here; not this time; not any more.

There was even a man—not sure what he was, Assistant to a Deputy-Minister or Director-General in some portfolio or other—who did not greet her when he was seated round a conference table; one of those in official positions who do not see unimportant people: a simple defect in vision. Which meant that she did not turn to the voice, thought it was someone else in the corridor who was being addressed, when this man was saying, as she recognised him drawn level with her —Will you come for a drink?— In a pause, he added her name: —You are Miss Blayne.— As if confirming an identity.

—I'm sorry . . . I didn't . . . —

They were being carried along by politely hurrying people, sticks caught in a river current. —Here's the bar.—

She was so unprepared that she trotted along with the man like a schoolgirl summoned. He and his appendage were greeted with the special attention accorded by waiters and barmen indiscriminately to any face known to be in Government. He rejected one table-nook and was immediately directed to a choice of others; only the stools at the bar were occupied. She could not remember his name and did not know how to open a conversation as his silence seemed to suggest she was expected to. The waiter came, the man looked to her: she ordered her usual brand of Scotch and he made it: —Two doubles and what is there— chips, nuts.— He sent the chips back because they were stale. Then he began to speak, address—yes, he had been, he was addressing her—now, with questions about what she had had to say, at her Administrator's request, in the meeting just ended. If he did not look at her or acknowledge her presence at these official sessions, it appeared that he—she unaware of this attention as he had shown himself of her existence—listened to her duly Agency-correct depositions. There had been a contentious discussion about the ratio of subsistence crops to cash crops, particularly those with potential for export, in rural development. He wanted to know how the Agency arrived at its recommended balance, and how, in other developing countries the rural people could be convinced that it was (he had the term ready from the Government's unwritten primer) the way forward.

She was in a bar with this composed, impersonal man, but she had two good swallows of whisky bringing her to smile across his distance. —Of course. You try telling someone to grow wholesome grain and potatoes when he wants to sell tobacco leaf and afford a TV or enough cash to buy an old car, new clothes! And what about the big money from drug crops, marijuana . . . —

But from his side, the conversation in the beer-reeking dingy nook built during colonial rule in nostalgia for an English pub was being conducted as a continuation of the afternoon meeting where the Agency's agenda (hidden agenda as the phrase-book defines these) and the Government's counterpart were trawling for accommodation. She managed, through contexts of his questions, to find out that he was Deputy-Director-General in the Ministry of Land Affairs, handman-of-the-Minister's-handman, the Director-General. When the waiter hovered, he waved him away over the two emptied whisky glasses; she wondered whether he expected her to acknowledge this session was over, and rise, or if that would seem presumptuous—Agency protocol must respect official precedence in such decisions. But she could tactfully indicate that it was time to leave: there was something acceptably conclusive about her referring her host to her Administrator: —I know Mr Henderson would be only too pleased to talk to you about our successes—and our problems! Afghanistan, Colombia . . . nothing he hasn't experienced—

They walked out together. The corridor, like the whisky

glasses, had emptied; they said goodnight and then as if remembering the most elementary protocol, he offered his hand to her.

Roberta Blayne told her Administrator that the Deputy-Director in the Ministry of Land Affairs had approached her with some further questions about the subsistence crop–cash crop debate; Henderson said they might make it their business to cultivate the man, he hadn't been prominent in the debate that afternoon, nor was heard from much at other sessions where you'd expect him to speak up, mh?—but one didn't know who was or was not influential behind the scenes in the cabinet. What was his name again?

A Saturday ten days later she was drying her hair when the phone rang and a secretarial voice informed her that the Deputy-Director in the Department of Land Affairs was on his way to visit her; was this convenient. But it was a statement, not a question. She had only just combed out her hair and wriggled bare feet into sandals when she heard a horn and from her window saw the man who woke her with tea and polished the floors, heels flung up as he raced to open the gates. A black car of the luxury models provided for officials just below ministerial level came crunching over the gravel, delivered the Deputy-Director of Land Affairs at the front door, and was directed by the houseman round to the yard.

She had the door open: there he was, Deputy-Director Gladwell Shadrack Chabruma, still formally dressed in a suit as he would be on official occasions, although it was Saturday. They shook hands once more. She led him to the livingroom. —You may have been in this house some other time—when Chuck Harris was the Agency's man here, with his team? You probably know the place, anyway.—

—Thank you. No, I did not have the occasion to come to this particular house, of course I knew Mr Harris and his people. I was in the Ministry of Agriculture during that period.—

—Well that must have been an ideal preparation, for Land. I'll get us some tea—you'd prefer coffee?—

—Whatever. It is a good background to have, that I agree, but the problems are different, yes, agriculture's—they come after the question of ownership of the land—

She was at the passage leading to the kitchen. But when this man of few words at working breakfasts and meetings did begin to talk he expected no interruption. She had to hover there.

—The Ministry where I was . . . was deployed . . . before—Agriculture, we came up against it all the time, excellent opportunities from the point of view of developing better farming practices, introduction of new crops and so on—the best expertise from other countries, the agencies and all that. But to introduce this on little plots everywhere, all over, too small for anything but subsistence farming—where is the land.—

—Oh we understand only too well in what my boss calls our outfit—we know that until the land's reclaimed that was taken from you in colonial times, the larger agricultural projects we advise can't go further than enthusiasm . . . Even yours, if we convince you they're good . . . That's why we have to look at projects we're able to get going now. The community ones people from those little plots can work on together—oh you've heard it all before—

She got away to order the tea, words trailing after her.

In the kitchen she found a uniformed driver and two men with the heavy shoulders, armed belts, and discreet communication contraptions in their ears—the display of bodyguards as the spread tail is the display of a peacock—seated round the kitchen table already drinking tea from the houseman's big mugs. The houseman was animatedly hostly over them but set about at once putting some relic of a starched lace mat on a tray for the other serving he would bring to her and the occasion of her distinguished guest, a man from the Government.

The guest appeared to be still with the statement left behind in the passage, ignoring her ritual of serving him tea, before he spoke. It could have been unease, or the self-confidence of status. He had the gift of the closed face that blackness, in her experience, enviably makes obscure. The so-called inscrutability of the Chinese was no match. He was very black, no taint of colonial dilution in the blood, there.

—You are satisfied with the progress?—

Did he mean of the country or the Agency's efforts within it? Safer to take it as reference to the Agency. —How could we be? Always want to achieve more, feel we could have done more. Progress is slow . . . our approach is to learn what's needed, right where we are—

—How does it compare?—

So he had meant his country. Had he been sent by someone—another hidden agenda—to get something out of an unsuspecting female, not in a high position but in the know, close to the Administrator of funds.

Not so easy with this one, he was going to find; and let him wonder if she was too innocently stupid to suspect what he was after, or too alertly experienced in such devious politicking to let him get at it. She produced the Agency's stock responses, reassuring appreciation of the Government's sharing of objectives, unchallengeable knowledge of its own people, vital element of their history in influencing, guiding the possibilities of the present etc. All this compared, she would say, rather favourably (her tongue's quick caution had held back 'very') with other territories where the Agency had operated.

—And you were always with him, so for you also, you know his impressions.—

—Always, no. But in the last few years. I've been fortunate enough to learn a lot from him. Experience with him.—

And for the half-hour or less the subject—whatever it really was—went no further. He followed the necessary preliminary of hitching the cuff of his striped shirt that protruded at the correct length from his jacket sleeve, looking at his watch. —I have a meeting.—

He named another province, a two-hour journey away.

She called to the kitchen, for him, and in the moments of silence as they walked together to the front door they could hear the loud and laughing farewells between his driver and bodyguards and her houseman.

As he was about to step into the car brought round with a flourish from the yard, he turned. —I hope I did not disturb your weekend.—

The protocol came instinctively to her, she left the verandah, protesting, her hand out for his.

The livingroom held the low emptiness left by a transient occupation in which there was no meeting: the only one was the political appointment for which the man had stopped by on the way. But the houseman Tomasi was so elated by the official visitors he had entertained that he kept up a bass hum as he went about his work, doing something tympanically noisy in the kitchen.

It was only when she was driving to lunch with the Hendersons on Sunday, she suddenly remembered: that afternoon after the strictly single glass of whisky she had told the man that her Administrator would be pleased to have a talk with him; but Alan Henderson had not asked her to arrange an appointment at the Deputy-Director's convenience, and she had not reminded him of this. *That* was the unspoken message of the visit on Saturday!

She and her Administrator were playfully but firmly forbidden, by his wife, to chew over, as she put it, Agency stuff on Sundays, but while the Administrator's Assistant and her boss were sitting out during a mixed doubles at tennis she took the chance to tell him of the Saturday visit—of course the man wanted to know why the Administrator of the Agency hadn't approached him, was offended. Her dereliction of duty, really! —That's what I'm for, to see that you take the hints passed on to me!—

They were being called to the court. —No aid in the doubles!— A cry from his wife Flora. They leapt to their feet in mock alacrity.

Roberta Blayne hastened with the genuine thing to call the Deputy-Director's secretary and arrange the date and time when the Administrator would come to his office. Or would the Deputy-Director care to lunch with him?; whichever.

Alan Henderson was back in New York for a special briefing at headquarters and she had had a week of overwhelming work, dealing with what it was long tacitly agreed she could do as well as he, and stalling responses to requests that must await his return. She was on the telephone to him across the seven-hour time difference when she might have hoped to get some sleep. The computer screen, voice mail, e-mail, the cell phone's summons: when she finally did get back to the house she could not tolerate another four walls and found herself walking round, up and down, the garden—so enclosingly over-grown that she felt like some animal let out only into an exercise pen. There was a party she was invited to at the witty lawyer's with Flora Henderson, that Saturday night; she felt too tired to expect to enjoy herself but didn't want to disappoint Flora. In the morning she was half-heartedly looking through her clothes for something to wear that evening when the telephone rang. Early in the Southern Hemisphere, middle of the night, across the world; wouldn't be Alan, thank God.

There was the voice that seemed always to be addressing someone else: *who, me? Roberta Blayne, yes, speaking.* As if it could be other, unless that of the houseman Tomasi; or does the man think I don't live alone.

Would she like to come out in the country, see something of the rural Eastern area, —I don't think you have been.—

—Oh. Oh . . . When.—

—Today. I can fetch you from your house at nine-thirty. Or ten. What you like. It's quite a long way, not good to leave too late.—

He had had his meeting with the Administrator before Alan left for America, so surely that was enough contact. But suddenly the idea of getting out of the glowering matted garden into space, grass and sky, the scent and feel of air not over-breathed by people and blasted by airconditioning—the appropriate responses came, never mind for whom. —Lovely, love to get away, thank you, can we make it ten? I didn't have much sleep last night, got up late . . . —

Instead of the elegant silk trousers for the party she pulled out a pair of jeans less worn than those of her usual weekend wear; leather lace-ups instead of sandals—'the country' might include some rough walking, at least she hoped so.

He came driving himself in his own car. Also a luxury model but an older one and he was alone. The dark three-piece suit had been shed; Flora knew the wife of the local Indian, *Expert Tailor & Gentleman's Outfitter* who made a lot of money in custom-cutting this only slightly varied uniform for parliamentarians. The Deputy-Director wore khaki pants and a blue shirt, open-necked, but with his unchanged air of formality. He held the passenger door wide for her as she settled herself chattering, and Tomasi, clearly delighted at the reappearance of the important visitor, stood to watch the car leave through the gates of what was his domain whatever transients from the Agency might occupy it.

—In your place, your home, there in England, you live in the country, you like the country life so much, Miss Blayne?—

She laughed. —You can't spend the day giving me a breather, calling me 'miss'—please, I'm Roberta.—

He did not try it out until they had been driving for a while and it was clear—his tone made it clear—that this usage was not to be taken as unwonted familiarity. His supposition that field trips with the Administrator would not have been in the direction taken now, was correct; that was a suitable opening for him to give her information about the countryside they were travelling, the people who lived there—migration from the West because of floods a few years ago, migration from the South because of more recent drought, cattle country here, maize on the plain, baboons, yes (she thought she saw something move on the rocks) and even a leopard sometimes, in the hills. But mostly shot out.

—Fur coats for ladies in Europe?—

—I wouldn't say that. We have poaching pretty much under control in this area. The big game was really finished, anyway, long ago, the old days when the British were here. Many years of their governors' hunting parties.—

Denunciation of the colonial period, whether bitter or merely derisive, was a stock subject in social exchanges among Government and other dignitaries' circles, to which the Agency often contributed. Alan Henderson could always raise a laugh along with a glass: —Thank my lucky stars I'm not a Brit!— It didn't count that his Assistant apparently was; she didn't matter. She had been in Deputy-Director Gladwell Shadrack Chabruma's presence on such occasions; this present passing remark about the colonial governors was near as he had ever come to bitter historical judgments. Due to his being habitually the man of few words? Or it could be a sign of strength of character: no indulgence of dwelling on the past for every lack in the present; perhaps even the largesse of forgiveness—the same 'Brits' were being offered the grace of retribution by their providing more 'soft' loans. The way forward. She didn't know the man; not even to the extent she felt she knew some of his colleagues by professional attention to the views most of them volubly expressed.

There were villages of the very kind where the Agency entered into local projects with the inhabitants; she could tell him, if he happened not to know of it, of the successful brick-making that employed women whose husbands had lost their jobs due to the closure of an old coal mine—the women provided bricks for the men to build a school and a clinic, and had begun to sell surplus production to make a living for themselves. The way forward. Well . . . inch by inch. This time he was the one to assure of suitable appreciation; land acquisition was on a grand scale, a difficult operation (for the first time he allowed himself a glance away from the road, at her, and she understood an unspoken reference to the forced occupation of white farmers' land by the people in a neighbouring country). —Small is beautiful. Also. Isn't that it.— And he smiled, she saw in profile, his attention on the road. Not far on there was a village with a store crouching under a broad sign BAMJEE'S DRINK COCA COLA PETER STUYVESANT. —What would you like?— He pulled up the car.

She was fine, didn't want anything, thank you.

The children who were the frieze of her actions, her life, on Agency assignments everywhere, gathered slowly round the car while he was in the store. They are always the same children. Their black skin as if sandpapered grey, their leaking noses and shy giggles. One or two come up to her window silently; it is their way of begging. What could she have asked him for? What need could she possibly have, before these. It is the policy of the Agency not to give handouts; charity is not an answer, although caritas is part of an answer when you open your mouth and out comes 'empowerment' 'development'. She was off duty; the man was not wearing his Deputy-Director's garb: she fumbled in her locally-woven straw bag and brought up some useless small change to give before he appeared from the store.

Bottle-heads winked and the serrated topknot of a pineapple poked out of plastic bags he was carrying. In the rear-view mirror she saw him stacking the trunk. When he got into the driver's seat he handed her a bottle of soda. —No mineral water . . . I'm sorry no cup, glass—

And now she thought it ridiculous, even rude, not to be using his name, if without permission. —Who needs a glass, thanks so much Gladwell—I realise I'm thirsty after all.— She tipped back her head and drank as he drove; paused, wiped the mouth on her shirt and offered the bottle to his hand on the wheel, but he merely lifted splayed fingers, kept the hand in place. —I had something in the shop.—

She wanted to say, I don't have any communicable disease, but he was not a person with whom one could joke. (As if one could joke about anything 'communicable' these days when a new pestilence threatened intimacy.) Instead she asked him where they were making for—or was this going to be a circular drive, nowhere in particular. No, they were going to a place, there was a place where an uncle of his lived, he had some papers for him, something to arrange. —An old man doesn't understand these matters. It's on the edge of the forest, mopani trees, you know those? Illala palms.—

—A village?—

—Not really. Outside the village.—

—What does he grow? Does he farm cattle?—

—It's not a cattle farming area. They can't cultivate. His sons work in town and send some money to the old ones.—

There was a one-room-sized brick house with a tin roof and three or four satellite huts whose thatch hung like grey falling hair. In such a place, the car seemed grown twice its size, the sun clashing off its brilliant black surface. The Agency's scarred station wagons she was used to arriving in were less blatant. An old man in a sagging dark jacket and trousers (could it be a cast-off parliamentary suit handed down) and a woman so round and heavy in her skirts she might have been the African version of a Russian doll with many clones of descending size inside her, came out of the house and warm greetings and exclamations were exchanged. His passenger didn't know the language but gathered these were praise of the member of the family who was in Government.

She stood by smiling, as on a field trip with her Administrator. The couple had shown no reaction at the arrival of a white accompanying the Deputy-Director; no doubt a Government man, one of their own, could command a white secretary. Their member of the Government introduced her first in their language, and when the old man responded in English, Pleased to meet you, madam: —This lady—she's from the aid people in America who are helping the Government in our country.— So now the distinction of the visit was doubled, for the old couple. But with dignity of his own the old man gestured to his house— the Deputy-Director responded with some interjection that led to his taking his uncle reverently by the arm, and the two of them fetched three chairs and a stool from the house.

—The English lady enjoys the sun.— The old man bowed to her. His wife brought tea—the fellow-woman gesture of rising to help was met with an authorative side-to-side of the head on the ample neck. The guest took no part in the conversation, either, because the old woman spoke no English and the men seemed to have much to discuss in their own language; but Roberta Blayne was accustomed to this, too, in her role as the Administrator's side-kick, alertly at ease, speaking up only when it was indicated by the sign language between them (a certain way he shrugged a shoulder almost imperceptibly in her direction) she ought to. Papers were signed, with the Deputy-Director leaning over the old man's shoulder as the pen moved in a hand mummified by toil—that was the biblical word that came to her as the one for subsistence farming; while the men talked she learnt with her gaze around what the old couple's life was: a hand-pump stood crookedly, there was a small patch of maize, white-plumed close to the house, the nagging complaint of a tethered goat, some potato plants, withered cabbages like severed heads and a few plump orange pumpkins. The sun was fierce; they moved into shade. Green handgrenades hung from the branches of the avocado tree.

This was, after all, her outing; she rose, smiling. —Gladwell, I think I'm going to go for a walk. Up to that hill over there, see the view.—

He broke off what he was saying to his uncle, head vehement. —No, no. You can't walk around out there, there can be land mines still not cleared. No.—

It was as if the queer image that had come to her—fruit in the guise of weapons had been a warning. In countries where not long ago there had been one of those civil wars supplied with such weapons for both sides by foreign countries with 'agendas' of their own, the violence lies shallowly buried. The Agency had had enough experience of that. So the stout rubber-soled hiking boots were not to be put to use.

As the honoured guests were about to leave, he brought the plastic bags from his car and carried them into the house. Only then. She found this unexpectedly delicate, certainly in this man; he hadn't wanted the old couple to start insisting that the guests share what was meant for themselves. The old man and woman followed him, protesting happily. The woman came back with a knife in her hand and cut down two avocados, presented them to the woman from the aid agency.

She weighed them, heavy, one in either hand, thank you, thank you.

Now they were fruit.

In the car she placed them on the rear seat. He seemed to contemplate a moment on the suitability of the gift. —They will get ripe.—

She forgot to take them with her when he dropped her at her house. It was dark, she'd had to shout for the houseman Tomasi, who ignored the horn, to come and unlock the gates.

On Sunday she went with Flora to fetch Alan Henderson from the airport, back from New York. He was elated. —We've a whole new allocation of funds!—

—Tell, tell!—

—One-and-a-half million more.—

His Assistant and his wife celebrated him: you're a wizard, a Midas, how'd you do it, what'd you tell them. —We-e-ll—this country is stable, right—by standards of the newly emergent economies, it's ditto democratic, on the way there, anyway, and if we want to help keep it on its feet, we must do more to promote good governance, while projects must be totally co-operative, real money must be put into them, theirs and ours—

His colleague knows that 'specific project choices' are what they'll have to adapt, finagle, beyond fine intentions.

—And how'd they receive our *well-documented* doubts about funds for IT?—

—That was the tough one. They came up with their solu-

29

tion: funds to supply generators for community centres and so on where we know there's no local power plant. How feasible that is . . . we'll work on it. They still see this continent left behind to be the Dark Continent again, Mister Kurz he dead, unless IT comes *first*—even before houses, schools and clinics. Maybe they're right . . . On line into the world and what's missing will follow. And there's enthusiasm over our AIDS education strategy. They're waking up over there in AmeroEurope to see if the new Plague isn't stopped nothing much else we do will matter . . . that's what's going to bring about a Dark Continent in our age of globalisation.—

Over lunch he asked what she'd been up to.

As if he hadn't been kept only too well informed: —Minding the store for you. Plenty of problems I didn't trouble you with, though.—

Flora was carving a leg of lamb. —Not now, not now, in your office on Monday.—

—But I did have a break. Out in the country yesterday. The Deputy-Director of Land Affairs turned up and took me for a drive, he had some chore and I suppose looked for useful company. Did you know there're still land mines not cleared in the Eastern province?—

—Good grief, I'd been told it was all clear except for the frontier in the West! We'd better look into that with Safety and Security—Defence, maybe. Was he fishing again, an Agency sardine or two to dish up for his boss's reports to the Minister? As he was doing with me, as well, when we lunched. We'll never get these guys in Government to understand we have to keep out of political issues—or seem to. As if sinking a borehole in this village before that doesn't become political. What does he think about IT—or does he only utter on land? If you see him again, bring it up; he must sit at all manner of closed meetings with his Director, he must have a general idea of what the Government's prepared to do, we have to gather what we can to work on for co-operation from it. They can't expect to leave it all to the big network donors . . . as you noticed, *their* stocks have gone wa-ay down, anyway.—

The Hendersons put Deputy-Director Gladwell Shadrack Chabruma and his wife along with the name of the Director of Land Affairs himself on the list for a cocktail party marking the Agency's decade of service in Africa. The Director brought his wife, his Deputy came alone. As if there was no wife; but there's always a wife, somewhere. When Roberta, co-host with the Hendersons, greeted him she was about to add as a pleasantry, I forgot the avocados, but did not. Turned with other pleasantries to a man from Home Affairs, arrived with the Minister of Welfare (rumours of another kind of affair, there) who always tried to manoeuvre her sisterly into a corner with some urgent situation of women that must be brought to the attention of the Agency.

These first weeks of Alan Henderson's return were taken up in collaboration with the local World Health Organisation representative in meetings arranged for a senior man from WHO headquarters who was touring the continent in a campaign against HIV AIDS. There were visits to rural counselling centres set up in army surplus tents and to an old hospital still known by the name of a deceased English queen, now a hospice—euphemism for the last of the Stations of the disease. The Agency Administrator's Assistant had had to face, and walk away from, to life—starvation in Bangladesh, in India, not just the living human head resculptured by it, but its final power manifest, wreaked upon the feet, the skeleton of feet no longer for standing, the feet, the hands, the hands the very last web-hold on existence. People deployed on the ground (as opposed to those tours of duty looking down from cloud-high windows of metropolitan headquarters) are like doctors, they must do what they have to do without the fatality of identification with sufferers. But in this red-brick relic of imperial compassion for its subjects the long-established discipline become natural to her failed; suddenly was not there. She groped for it within herself; the anguish of the bodies on beds and mats entered in its place. She could not look, she *had to look*, at the new-born-to-die and the rags of flesh and bone that were all that was left of the children they were to become if they did survive weeks, months, maybe a year. Food and clean water (the succour ready to be provided on other tours of duty): useless here.

Silenced by what they had seen, the official group was taken to a Holiday Inn where the Agency had arranged a private room and coffee was served. She was hearing as echoes sounding off the walls the practical responses to—what? Incurable. Something incurable in the nature of human life itself, taking many forms of which this was the latest, arising, returning in endless eras and guises—disease, wars, racism. That's how people come to believe—have to believe—in the existence of the Devil along with God, Capital Initials for both. How else? How else answer why. But what there was in that place was not ontologically incurable! Just that a cure was not yet discovered. *Preventable.* That was the succour, in the meantime! Research facilities, preventive education—that was what, under the mantra of diffused tapes repeating pop songs, the people who were *doing something about these* were arguing, as the coffee revived blood run cold. And that was the code she belonged to: whatever there is, the ethic is do something about it. But she couldn't respond when her Administrator, with his usual consideration of the worth of her views, looked to see if she was going to speak.

The official car drew up at the gates just as she arrived back at the house. Dismay difficult to overcome: not this afternoon, end of this day! Draw the curtains pour yourself a whisky, no-one but the face, familiar in this delegated house, this tour of duty, of the attendant Tomasi.

Nothing for it but to blast the horn for Tomasi to come and open the gates—and dismay gave way to embarrassment, the blast sounded exasperated, she had the duty of a polite show of welcome, at least. As the gates were opened she waved a hand to signal the car to precede hers. The Deputy-Director of Land Affairs was deposited at the front door and his car proceeded once again round to the yard. She left hers and produced a smile to greet her guest.

Tomasi the sprinter was already opening the front door. Once she and Gladwell Shadrack Chabruma were in the living-room she excused herself: —May I dump my papers and tidy myself up, we've been about out of the office all day. Please—be comfortable.—

He will have heard her flushing the loo, water coming from the old squeaking taps as she washed, she did not look at herself in the bathroom mirror. Hadn't made himself comfortable.

There in his parliamentary dress he was standing as if he had just entered. —Come.— She turned to the sofa; while he seated himself, she indeed drew the curtains and opened the cupboard where the hospitality bottles were.

—It's too late for tea, don't you agree. Gladwell. What'll it be?—

—Whatever you are having.—

—Whisky? Soda, water?—

—I prefer soda.—

She drew up a little table for their drinks and joined him on the sofa. —We have a visitor from WHO in New York, we've been taking him around with people from the Ministry of Health, some from Welfare.—

—It is good when these principals come, see for themselves. Sometimes.—

—And other times?—

—They don't understand what they see, what it means; what we are doing.— One of his pauses. —They're seeing something else they bring along with them. What is it, the word . . . when I was a student at University of Virginia—a paradigm. Yes.—

Sometimes.

The curt proviso caught at her abstracted attention. The few occasions they had met, even in the opportunities of the week-end drive, he had not allowed himself any uncertainties. Now from this small indication that this official was also a man with doubts came the release coffee at the Holiday Inn had not brought her.

—I shouldn't be doing this job.—

Spoken suddenly for herself. But as if overheard by both—

34

the man was here so it must have been for him, too. —We were at that new water purification plant . . . two clinics they fund. And the old Queen Mary Hospital. You know.—

—Their AIDS programme.—

—WHO's and ours, the Agency.—

—You have had a very busy day. Roberta.—

And she was the one who had not seen what there was to see: here was a reassuring presence seated in physical solidity, affirming her worth, the correctness of the three-piece suit a sign of order—like the gown of a judge in the discipline of the law, a surgeon in his white coat—in a shaking world. A man in command of himself. Strong perfectly articulated hands enlaced at rest on his knees.

—It was unbearable. You should go—no, don't, don't go, it's what no-one's meant to see, how can I say, the processes, what happens after death and it's supposed to be buried away, but it's all there—living. The babies just born and that means beginning to die, there in front of you.—

In profile she saw his mouth drawn stiffly, eyebrows contracted. That he did not look at her made it possible for her to control the stupid, useless indulgence of tears.

He picked up his glass and drank, then stirred slightly, towards her. —I told you not to walk out because of land mines still there, my uncle's place. His youngest was home for school holidays and went with his dog to shoot a bird for his mother's pot and he was blown up. Both legs gone. Sixteen years. He died. They can't plant their fields.—

When the man had left she didn't know whether he had meant to reproach her weakness, or comfort her with the proof—seen it for herself—that the old couple continues to live surrounded by the Death that had killed their son, lying in wait for them to step upon it.

The tour of the WHO representative ended. Roberta Blayne and her Administrator took up their usual activities until the next partner in development came. She was doing her job. In the social life promoted by Flora Henderson beyond official entertaining and being entertained (enough, enough aidshoptalk) the bachelor woman was always in the company of couples. She danced with other women's husbands; no woman seemed to fear her. She couldn't consider herself lonely, and the work was among the most fulfilling she had ever been assigned to, since Alan Henderson used her particularly in meetings where, in accordance with the Agency's Mission Statement, local communities' ideas of what they most needed—dams, access roads to markets, chicks and fingerlings to begin poultry- or fish-farming, roofing and desks for a new school—were to be joint projects with them. Many of those chosen by people to speak for them were women; somehow she created confidence: surely a woman would listen to them?—but the men respected her, too, an official position counters many traditional prejudices. Her Administrator would remark to Government officials, Roberta's learning the language, you know, often she doesn't need an interpreter! She would protest—she certainly did! But the fact that his Assistant was taking the trouble, in a tour of duty that lasts only a couple of years, to learn the main language of the country reflected well upon the Agency. Often the community would give her some small gift (no vicuna coat bribe—the Agency allowed acceptance as a token of trust)—a carved wooden spoon, woven straw bags, a clay pot; the house she'd been assigned to began to take on the signs of homely possession that come with objects which have their modest personal history.

The black car of the luxury model provided for the second echelons of Government office-bearers was in the yard—perhaps once a week, could be any day. The driver and bodyguards installed in the kitchen.

The Deputy-Director of Land Affairs was the one acquaintance among many in her job (she knew their names, faces round conference tables, gossip about them, by now) who had become a special kind of acquaintance; his presence at least claimed that. They progressed from exchanges and courteous argument about current events in the country and the continent, inevitably, as people do when such talk runs out, to link observations from the past: when I was young, when I was a kid, I remember I thought it would be, it was . . . and to offer experiences of childhood background. Without any confidentiality, of course. These ordinary anecdotes are common currency.

But you are what you were.

There, then, the experiences don't meet; he began minding his father's cattle, classic for a government career in Africa, she was at a girls' school in an English cathedral town, the bells pealed while the basketball was aimed, the cattle lowed as they were driven under the herdboy's whip. He had been to a mission school, then a college in some neighbouring African country from where there came his scholarship to America. He had once mentioned a university. University of Virginia, wasn't it? Here, experience could be shared; well, she had studied for a year in the USA, exchange programme with an English university. He had wanted to go on to the Kennedy School of Government at

Harvard; it was part of the limits of contact he apparently always set himself that he did not offer the sequel to the intention. She had learnt not to fill his silences, but sometimes there was the vacuum's pressure to continue. Out of politeness he would have to make some sort of explanation.

—I was married, at home. Away a long time, I had to come back. Children.—

—They must be grown up now? Satisfaction to you . . . It's a trade-off, I suppose. I was married, but no children, unfortunately. Or maybe fortunately as there was a divorce. But I wonder if you really missed much, Harvard, I mean. You've gone through another kind of school of government, haven't you, right here.—

—We are all learners in the world. But academic things in a c.v., they impress people.—

—In government careers? At high level? I wouldn't have thought so. The President hasn't got a Harvard degree, not even a less grand university one from overseas, far as I know.—

—There are other qualifications to make up.—

He smiled at her in pride, lest she lure him to a lapse into criticism of the Head of State. —He was one of our first leaders in our war of liberation . . . he is a man who has not abandoned our culture the same time as he can take on the world. You know.—

—What are the children doing? Anyone interested in going into politics, like Dad?—

—Studying.— Subject closed.

One evening they had a second whisky and time had passed so unnoticed that she suggested some supper. The driver and bodyguards were already being fed maize meal and stew when she went to the kitchen to see what she and Tomasi could offer.

Over canned soup and cold chicken he told her of a farm in the Southern Province. —Your own farm?— Yes, he had a farm. (Doesn't everyone in government acquire a farm or farms, don't ask about how, nothing to do with the questions of land redistribution; but this was none of her business, certainly not at her own table with a guest.)

The next time the black car brought distinction to Tomasi's yard the Deputy-Director of Land Affairs invited her to visit his farm the coming weekend. When she told him there were two gatherings she was obliged to attend he merely substituted: —The weekend after, then.—

—Oh I don't want to spoil your plans, Gladwell, please—

—It's the same for me. I go all the time.—

So that is home, the family home, not the official residence (to which she has never been invited) that must be in the suburb of guard-houses manned before swimming-pool and tennis-court endowed gardens, where Government office-bearers and foreign diplomats lived. She looked forward with mild curiosity to meeting the wife and family. He must belong somewhere else outside the parliamentary suit—as he did with the old uncle and aunt, that glimpse she'd had of him in personal mufti. The black car was at the gates early, not unexpected of this stickler for all disciplines. She recognised one of the bodyguards doubling as driver; perhaps, unlike the destination of the other outing on which she'd accompanied the Deputy-Director, the area they were bound for in this vast country presented some possible threat which made the discreet, disguised-by-function presence of at least half his usual Security a precaution? So she and Gladwell were together on the back seat, very comfortable, he had no need to give any attention to the road, his man at the wheel had the air of a horse making surely for the stable.

It was far away. They rose and descended round a mountain pass, and caused people in two country towns to stare back at the majestic car's glossy blackness as the populace in distant times and far countries must have watched a royal carriage go by. In the third town he stopped (the other journey, he'd paused at a roadside store), this time before the town's landmark, a supermarket, and went in attended by the driver-bodyguard, perhaps only to carry provisions. She had her own secreted in her largest straw bag. The shaming resort to charity: a dose of sugar in place of an answer to the state of beggary. The children were there, the same children. She handed out a pack of sweets. The bodyguard and his charge returned loaded with food—must have been a long list from the wife. Then his man was in attendance on a visit to a liquor store behind the battered iron-pillared-and-roofed pavement that was the style of old frontier towns—along with the shopkeeper's Jewish name was pioneer immigrant provenance: I. SARETSKY EST. 1921. Bottles clanked in the trunk as the car moved off and the driver-bodyguard was instructed in their language to halt and rearrange his packing of provisions. Once more, refreshment had been brought for her; this time it was imported mineral water.

They talked between comfortable intervals—unlike his imposed silences—watching the country go by. The candelabra aloes were in bloom, flaming votive offerings to the ultimate cathedral that is the late winter sky when the heat has come, as it does, before the rains, a scouring to the bone that needs a term other than the one named Spring in Europe. The Cultural Attaché of the British had remarked to her at dinner last week, August's the cruellest month, not T. S. Eliot's April.

They came to the kind of terrain where activity by man has made savannah of what once was forest. Sparse scrub was nature's attempt to return among weathered rubble, half-buried rust-encrusted unidentifiable iron parts, even a jagged section of a wall where foundations traced by weeds outlined what might have been a building. Beyond some sort of slag heaps a rise where the picked-over remains of what must have been elaborate structures—houses?—of a considerable size, in scale with the giant hulks of fallen trees too heavy to have been carted away for firewood, still made their statement as an horizon. In other parts of the country she had seen farmsteads abandoned by whites pillaged for whatever might be useful; nothing of this extent. —What was here?—

—Used to be a mine. Long time ago. Before.—

—Copper?—

—Yes.—

—But what happened? Why isn't it still worked?—

—I don't know. Maybe the ore was finished—but in the war they say it was attacked and flooded, underground, the pumps were smashed. You can ask the Minister of Mines; the Buffalo Mine.—

There was a great deal of entertaining up at the Manager's house, weekends. On Monday morning a member of the kitchen and ground staff whose job it was set off to walk fifty miles to town with the master's note for the liquor store. A case of Scotch whisky. The man walked back with twelve bottles in the case on his head, arriv-

*ing Friday. Every Friday. The feat was a famous dinner-party story,
each weekend: that's my man—what heads they have, eh, thick as
a log.*

A stop at the last town to buy supplies the driver-bodyguard
loaded. I. SARETSKY EST. 1921. A case of Scotch whisky.
Twelve bottles on the head. That's my man. Thick as a log. That's
my man.

Buffalo Mine.

The name is a hook, the anecdote comes up with it. (The
driver-bodyguard has reduced speed in response to her movement, upright in her seat looking back at the site.)

First time in Africa? First time yes India Bangladesh Afghanistan not here.

Not only a dinner-party story of the long dead. *What an old
rogue, but such style! They don't make them like that anymore. Tax
evasion's about the only territory of adventurers now.* A child half-
listening, an adolescent bored with the tradition of family fables
recounted to later generations, around other tables, about that
extraordinary character, the grandfather.

Been here before.

Not in her person. But in her blood-line. The history to
which she belongs. There it was—is—Buffalo Mine. One of the
houses that were up there on the rise she's looking at was where
the dinner parties heard the famous story, drank the whisky arrived every Friday. Every Friday head thick as a log.

—You know the Minister? I'll introduce you.— Gladwell is in
the position to obtain any privilege a curious visitor might wish.
—Enos can tell you all about these old places.—

She sank back in her seat as if dismissing a passing interest.

Nearby was her destination, their destination, the Deputy-Director's farm. She had had in prospect a solid Colonial-verandahed farmstead taken over: there, looking on wattle-fenced cattle kraals, mud huts, a troop of sheep and goats, chickens taking a dust-bath under roses gone wild, a scatter of children bowling old tyres, was a house set down out of the sky complete from California. The expanse of glass behind the patio preened in reflected splendour of the sun, a satellite dish held its great ear to the world. Close by was a structure she recognised as a powerful electricity generator. Men and women came out of the back of the house to the double garage whose fine wooden doors rolled away as the driver-bodyguard touched the electronic gadget in his hand. The people were servants or perhaps relatives (she had observed how poorer members of an official's family often served in both capacities), some hastened to unload the car, a woman in a flounced floral overall that needn't necessarily mean she was cooking or cleaning, but a mark of status, hugged the master of the house and brought her palms together in greeting to his guest. She was ready to meet the wife in the house and perhaps some of the couple's grown children—of course the wife would speak English—anyway the social capabilities of her own training were automatically at hand for all such encounters.

There is an unmistakable atmosphere of absence in rooms where only servants have come and gone in the course of their daily tasks; no-one to fill these rooms has left presence there. Perhaps the arrival is unexpected, his wife is in some other wing of this house. He was following his guest's usual hostly procedure when *he* visited *her*, pouring whisky taken from a cabinet where glasses hung upside down from their stems as in a smart bar; he had not gone to summon anyone.

—I'd like to meet your wife, first.— The protocol smile as she accepted her drink.

—She prefers town.—

—Oh that's a disappointment.—

—The children come sometimes.—

—Well I'll have to meet her in town, then.— It was a tentative claim to friendship of the kind she was used to, the bachelor woman taken into a family context.

They were served a four o'clock meal—the woman in the flowered outfit must have been forewarned, after all, to have ready. The whisky bottle came to the skating-rink shiny table they sat at in a room that led off the livingroom peopled only by framed photographs of weddings, sports teams and official occasions in which he was among the assembly. Lively voices out of sight indicated that the driver-bodyguard must be sociably at home in the kitchen just as he was in Tomasi's.

She tucked in to stew and wild spinach, helped herself, under the permissive wave of the host's hand, to the mound of stiff maize meal smoking vapour like a dormant volcano. There were wheels of sliced tomato arranged as a still life on a glass plate. He was controlledly annoyed to find there was to be no coffee (apparently forgotten when the purchases were made at the supermarket); she noticed then what must have been there all along in him, the attractive tilt of his eyebrows drawn upward at the inner corners enquiringly even when he was not—as now—irritated. A hieroglyph of vulnerability to be deciphered, if one were to be interested enough, in the closed self-possession of this functionary.

—Can I walk round your farm?— She caught herself out in time and did not add the assumption: No mines? This was something not for flippancy brought about by a full stomach and whisky at an unaccustomed time of day.

—You don't want some tea?— To compensate for the missing coffee. —I'll take you. You know I have horses—of course, you come from England, all the English like horses.—

So together they passed the cattle sheds and the old stone-walled sheep pen (there must once have been another kind of farmer on this land, with his memories of the Cotswolds, and a white-verandahed farmstead she had had in mind). Neat pyramids of cow dung dried and cut in squares for fuel were milestones where small dogs of their own unnamed breed lifted jaunty legs as they panted along. He pointed to the field of chili peppers ready for harvesting; she was intrigued: —They're red earrings hanging!— A flung arm showed his cattle grazing far off; there was maize stretching away as a head-high forest. —Three thousand bags this year, that's not bad . . . but this was many hectares planted, you have to have the land to get a commercial crop like that . . . This place was nothing. Weeds and rubbish. Like the other.—

This was the moment for her anecdote. *My grandfather owned that mine he lived there*—the present moment would grow over the past safely, organically, as the maize and blood-bright peppers and the russet and white pattern of the distant cattle repossessed the land that was colonial booty. But the moment had passed; they'd come to a paddock where three horses seemed, as horses do when they are approached, to be waiting. She said (of course) —They're beautiful.— And added —Specially the bay.—

He sucked his lips in round his tongue, used to making decisions for others. —Would you like to ride. She's a nice animal. The quiet one.—

—Oh I'd love to! Even one that isn't too quiet! I used to ride a lot, no chance now.—

—You see. I know the English.—

—You ride?—

He called out and a young boy appeared, was given an instruction.

—I also used to, when I was a kid, on the back of the old horse that pulled my father's cart. But now, no, I bought these for my son. He's in the States. His saddle's here.—

The boy saddled the bay and her host gave her a leg up to mount the tall horse. The forgotten sensation of co-operative power with the creature carrying her came immediately she set off, the old pleasure in the air swiftly parting against her face. Unexpectedly, he did not give any directions or instructions of where she might ride; she galloped, free, alongside the maize fields disturbing minute birds like clouds of insects, she rode over the open ground towards the cattle, waved at the herdboy squatting with them, she turned back towards the city-slicker house and swerved away to where she made out what must be him, although something about the figure was different, not only from the parliamentary-suited one but also from the one in mufti of sports shirt and pants. There was another man with him and as she neared she found they were bent over some sort of pump installation. Now, up on the horse, she was beside them. He was different; he had stripped off his shirt, hands stained with grease and dirt he rose bare-breasted. Nothing significant in a man naked to the waist, as there is when every magazine cover uses the evident evocation of bare-breasted females. But perhaps because this man was always so *fully dressed* in the abstract as well as the material sense, what was revealed couldn't have been guessed at. This torso seemed to belong to someone other in the gleaming beauty, sweat-painted, of perfectly formed muscle, the double path below pectorals, left and right, of smooth ribbing beneath lithe skin. Black. Simply black. No mark, no hairy pelt. Who is this man?

—Every time I'm here, it's some problem. Pump packed up.—

She laughed. (The problems of the *maison secondaire*.) She was sweating, too, her forehead gleamed hot and rosy.

—The ride was good?—

Wonderful, wonderful.

He took a shower. She was directed to what must be the wife's bathroom; a pink comb and an empty bath-oil bottle on the shelf, a gown hanging in folds like a crestfallen face.

They were having a farewell whisky on the patio—in the itinerary of her day's treat—about to leave for the long drive back when the woman in charge of the house burst out flustered. A rising tempo of exchange began between her and the host; he followed her into the house with a gesture of exasperation. But when he came back to the patio he was his composed self, distanced from whatever this problem was.

—The man's been drinking. My driver. They're having a big party there, all the time.—

—Drunk?—

—He can't drive.—

Not a tragedy. She spread her hands and cocked her head cheerfully. She was used to all sorts of necessary changes of arrangements, in the course of working journeys with her Administrator. —We can drive—you and I.—

—In the dark, at night. It's not safe.—

—Oh I don't mind, we'll be all right, sharing, I've often driven in rural areas at night.—

—Not the driving. It's not safe.—

Not safe. Ah yes, the drunk's not just a driver, he's a body-guard.

—He'll be back in his head in the morning. We can go very early. Is that okay for you? Sunday tomorrow—you don't have some appointment? I'm sorry.—

—Well I suppose . . . nothing else for it. I mean if there's risk, for you. No, I don't have anything particular planned . . . Nobody expects me. Nobody sits up for me.— She smiled to assuage his concern. —That's freedom.—

—I appreciate your attitude. Many women . . . —

The woman in charge of the house produced a tray with cold meats and bread and they drank whisky, talking 'development shop' in an indiscreet way, criticising, analysing this individual and that as they had never done (he would never allow himself to?) without the whisky, anywhere but hidden safe in the house that must have been a lit-up fantasy in ancient total darkness surrounding them. Not only the driver-bodyguard had made his escape, that night, from the restraints of official duty.

When both began to yawn uncontrollably he found it appropriate (every situation has its protocol) to rise from the sofa's fake leopard-skin velvet and decide —I'll show you where you can sleep.—

In the rhythm of their progress along a passage she told him—What a lovely day, and the ride—and he put an arm up around her shoulder, rather the gesture of a man towards a male friend.

There was no sign of whose room it was she was left in: the

character of the misplaced Californian house that there were rooms for purposes that did not match needs where it had been set down. It seemed to have been intended as some sort of spacious dressing-room, adjunct to other quarters behind a second door which was blocked by a bed. There were blankets and pillows, no sheets. But she had no provision of pyjamas, night-things, either; she was sitting on the bed a moment, contemplating this, the door to the passage still open, when he looked in to see if she wanted anything. She stood up to reassure, no, no, I'm fine, moving a few steps towards him to demonstrate self-sufficiency. He met her and whether she presented herself first or his arms went around her first wasn't clear; the embrace became long, as if occupying one of his silences. His mouth moved from hers over her face and neck and his hands took her breasts. When they were naked he left her briefly without a word from either and came back into the room with the condom concealed in his hand as he might carry a ballot paper in a parliamentary process. On the bed that seemed to belong to nobody the torso revealed beside the faulty irrigation pump came down on her fulfilling all its promise. Sometime between the pleasuring, this man of few words, in his new guise, spoke her name as a lover does. —Roberta . . . Like a boy's name, why did they call you . . . — —Because they'd wanted a boy.— And after a moment, a breathy half-laugh against his neck: —Why'd they call you Gladwell. Same thing? Wanted you to be something else. Make you a white Englishman.—

At six in the morning the driver-bodyguard had already brought the car round to the terrace, ready to go. He showed no sign of his night's debauch. She was to wonder some time afterwards if he really had been drunk. Or had been given instruction that he was; but then who could measure the unexpressed will, hers as well as her host's, that was ready for the pretext.

People in official positions, men and women with a public persona know how to accommodate officially unsuitable private circumstances for some sort of decorum within these positions and personae. Even someone with as low a level of official and public persona as Administrator's Assistant in an international aid agency knows this; along with computer competency and the protocols of tact and diplomacy in relations with the recipient country; another unspoken code. Aid personnel are not permitted to make personal attachments to local individuals on the premise that these might influence aid decisions; if they do indulge in such attachments—and they did—they are trusted to honour the Agency's objective integrity by following the rules of discretion on both sides—the individual's in exchange for the Agency's blind eye. For members of Government of course the circumstance is taken for granted—a man or woman in high office would be expected to have along with a luxury car and security guards, some woman, some man, for relaxation; faces outside the official portraits at home with the family.

The official car of the Deputy-Director of Land Affairs was often parked in the yard behind the house assigned by the Agency to the Administrator's Assistant. The driver and security guards sat in Tomasi's kitchen as habitués unremarked as any of his other friends. They might be called out and dismissed by their charge, the Deputy-Director, to leave the car and find their way home, return in the morning. Somehow though neither he nor she in their new-found rapport had to speak of it, neither would make love with the men talking and laughing in the kitchen.

She had only once before had a love affair abroad on a tour of duty, brief and in Europe in an hotel where the man arranged a room under a name other than his own (which the receptionist's eyes made clear was well-known). The man's wife was away and it was apparently his code of marital honour not to take a woman home in her convenient absence. But here, no doubt, there was the Deputy-Director's commonsense idea that there was no call for special arrangements—there's his farm, and the Agency house provided for the woman herself, alone. The guards and driver, the attendant Tomasi: they are there to serve needs, not to question whatever these may be; security has wide implications. Let them gossip and laugh, who knows what it might be about, in the kitchen; no-one's going to take notice of whatever they might pass on to others at their social level.

The Administrator and his wife Flora rarely came to his Assistant's bachelor woman house; it was so much more friendly to have her using as some sort of real temporary home the one Flora kept open to many, a household with food and drink and unquestioning welcome always just beyond the door, the young son plucking the guitar. Yet they must have guessed a new element had entered Roberta Blayne's tour of duty, even before this became tacitly recognised and generally accepted through certain signs in the conduct of Deputy-Director Gladwell Shadrack Chabruma. If Flora in her all-embracing but fixed impressions of a personality on first acquaintance noticed nothing, it is certain that Alan Henderson, working beside Roberta every day, and dependent on the results of their exchanged observations of

51

the people with whom they had to engage, was aware—and as only a man can be—of a warmed femaleness that emanates from a women who is being made love to, dormant in her before. He said nothing to his wife; put his private observation in the category of Agency matters that should fall into 'aid talk' which was, on her own dictate, not her business . . . But then as months went by and evidently the Deputy-Director gained confidence in the acceptance of his affair (maybe his colleagues in Government hierarchy even thought it might be useful: some woman from the aid Agency of which they had important financial expectations) he began to appear in public alone with Roberta Blayne. Flora, like others, became aware that her bachelor woman of retiring personality, not-so-young, was having an affair with a member of the Government. She was warned by her husband not to broach the subject. —But if Roberta talks to me? I mean it's out of the blue! Who would have thought he'd . . . that up-tight fellow . . . and if he did, one of the young interns in his office or some speakerine from TV, like the others pick, that would be what he'd go for, if at all—

Roberta didn't 'talk' to her, but as time passed Flora made clear with inoffensive remarks (Of course I don't suppose you'll come, you'll have better things to do this weekend) that she knew of the affair and was pleased about it, for her friend the bachelor woman's sake. Soon Roberta was able to respond quite naturally, yes, I'm going to the farm with Gladwell if he hasn't got some special meeting coming up on Saturday. It was mutually understood with the Hendersons that much as they would have liked it, and surely Roberta too, he was not invited with her to intimate dinners at the Henderson house—too much of a defiant sign to others present that this was a particular relationship.

When he came as of right to official parties there, both she and the hosts treated him on the same level of impersonal friendliness they did any other guest. There's a protocol for every situation.

At the President's celebration at State House on the anniversary of Independence Day she must have glanced over, without noticing, Flora *tête-à-tête* with someone in the crowd, a woman. Flora came up with the half-comic tolerant expression of having made an escape: —Good soul, I'm sure, but what can you talk about with her—when you get onto the standby, what are her interests, she tells you about her favourite TV soapie. Homebody of the new kind, the city peasant—you know the poor dears— Flora stopped herself; then the aside —That's Gladwell's wife. Must have married her very young and apart from producing a brood . . . she's sure no asset in furthering his career now.—

She looked across the room at the woman, as an intrusion on privacy; observing herself, rather, as the lover of the woman's husband, squeamish; old conventions wagging a finger at her. It was the only time they met—or rather didn't meet. He sometimes mentioned, in contexts where it was natural and inevitable, his wife: a car accident in which they'd both been slightly injured, subject come up when on one of the weekend trips to the farm the driver-bodyguard almost landed his passengers in a culvert (this time certainly did have a hangover).

There must have been some sort of accommodation with his wife; anyone, like Roberta Blayne, who has been once coupled knows there are many acknowledged sidetracks on the secret map of a marriage. Sometimes they met in a restaurant where he might be seen, by others in parliamentary suits, dining with a woman from the Agency personnel. His woman, no doubt. Many had theirs, if not in their company on that occasion. It was that sort of restaurant.

One day when she entered another restaurant he had chosen there was a young woman seated at the table with him. She hesitated a moment, whether she should approach, he saw her, lifted a palm, she came to it. He gave her name in introduction first. —Roberta Blayne. She is Assistant to Mr Henderson who heads the Agency here, now.— The girl half-rose with the casual acknowledgement of her generation and smiling, held out a hand to the woman standing before her. The hand was long, supple, ringed on fingers and thumb, nails painted fluorescent butterfly-wing blue; an attribute. She was a confidently attractive girl, her beauty arranged in contemporary high style—hair straightened and secured at the crown by a bobbing bunch of glossy curls to be bought in the shops, the liquid flash of slanting eyes, bold lips sculpted in purple-red. —Phila, my younger daughter, she's just back for a break from her law studies in Nottingham. Your country.— So the two women, his women, talked about England, the girl's impressions, what was endearing she said she found in 'the Brits', what was annoying, what in their ways made her laugh. —You miss England? You're English, aren't you?—

She supposed she was. But something of all the countries where there'd been tours of duty.

—How're you finding Africa? I've only realised since I've been living away what it's really like, here! My homeground, hometown. Weird! Really weird. My father doesn't like to hear that, he says I'm forgetting who I am. Fat chance—the Brits keep me aware of that. But seriously—or rather not seriously,

I'm having a great time.— She caught her father's hand, flirta-
tiously reassuring any disapproval in his silence. A silence which
otherwise was easy; his remarks to the girl now and then, over
the food, no suggestion that the situation of the three present
might evoke suspicion and another kind of disapproval: in the
daughter.

She wanted to ask—sometime—why he had wanted his
daughter to meet her, to reveal her, so to speak, to his family, his
real life—that is how she thought of it. While she was not sure of
what was hers, she was of his. The right time to ask never came.
Perhaps he had not thought of the threesome in the way she had
seen it; for him, simply some parental obligation to take his visiting daughter out to lunch.

If she had need to justify—exonerate—her presence at the
table it would have to be in acceptance that she was not the first
nor would be the last of the Deputy-Director's affairs. Outside
his real life.

What she knew was that she and this man were giving one
another what each needed. Love, yes, in one of its many complex
forms; one of the simplest. Not-so-young; what might be called
the cerebral aspect of her (she knew she was no great intellect but
she had a well-exercised intelligence of the workings of the contemporary world) first brought them together; he expected to
engage seriously with her, draw from her opinions other than
those he was supplied with officially, exchange different perceptions of motives, of what a newcomer saw happening here, his
country, and the world she had had experience of quite widely.

In love-making there came an eloquence beyond speech. And
this eloquence of pleasure brought her to the danger of confid-
ing—part of the release of orgasm, handing over what can be

used against you. In such a moment, the privacy that is like no other: —Buffalo Mine. You know, the day I asked, that day. My grandfather owned it and he ran it like a slave plantation. 1920s. He sent a man on foot all the way to that liquor store, still there, you stopped at in town, to fetch a case of whisky for his weekend booze party and the man walked all the way back with a case of whisky bottles on his head. Went on Monday and was back on Friday. Every Monday every Friday. My grandfather made a famous joke of it, my man, what heads they have, thick as a log.—

He said nothing. Suddenly tears of shame, old shame unshed, *what heads they have* came from her and trickled to his shoulder. He released an arm from their embrace and brushed at the shoulder as if something had alighted there; the fingers discovered their wetness.

—What is the matter.—

—What we did here. In my family. The rest of us. What liars we are, coming to these countries as if we hadn't ever been, marvelling at the *primitive*—oh yes it's a dirty condescending racist word don't ever use it but the sense of it's there even in our commendment, our reports, our praise—don't say it, *naïve obtuseness thick-headed*—oh the people's capacity to endure burdens, the *usefulness* of this capacity, sound basis for development, hard as a log the possession of the power of money over it that's my man— She could hear her raving whisper.

His voice in the dark a vibration through his breast. —Things like this happened long ago. Nothing to do with you. That's how they were. That's how it was with them. Those people. Such things . . . It was the tradition.—

They made love again and she sensed, from him, she must resist the desire to caress his head, pass her hand over its shape again and again to banish what cannot be changed, a past. Not even by development. She belongs, he belongs, to the present.

In every tour of duty that is going well there is a looming frustration that there will be recall, a new posting, another country, just when more time is needed to see projects fulfilled.

—What d'you think—should I ask for an extension? Would you stay?—

There was no innuendo in Alan Henderson's question; he was thinking of their effectiveness as a working team. And she answered on the same practical level, using Agency-speak. —If you believe we really could get those five rural projects to the stage of capability they should have if they're going to become viable under their own steam, when we do go. Worth a try, with New York?—

The Deputy-Director of Land Affairs knew—must have known—it was the business of Government to be ready for a change of the aid development team assigned to the country— that her tour of duty would end in a few months. She did not tell him her Administrator was applying for an extension. To her, this would somehow have taken away the integrity of her response to Alan Henderson; introduced an unacceptable factor in her code: commitment to her purpose in this country. For her to hope for the extension; that would make her the liar, descendant of liars. And as well she did not tell him. The Administrator's request was refused; he was already lined up for another post, another country. No doubt she was too unimportant for a decision of where she would be 'deployed' to be made in advance of her return to headquarters. She and Alan Henderson redoubled their work to leave what they knew as a sustainable achievement behind them, and the hours and days of effort without a sense of time alternated intensely with nights when an official car was hidden in the Administrator's Assistant's yard, and the Sundays she was riding horses on the farm of the Deputy-Director of Land Affairs. The California house had come to life within its alien shell as two people talked, ate and drank, made love there. Her shampoo was in the bathroom. There were no reproachful ghosts to be met when they slept in the big bed, a couple's bed. The wife prefers town. The only troubling matter for Roberta Blayne was a growing attachment to the farm. It was as if no-one had ever owned it before, because attachment, love for a place, is like love for a human being, it brings that place, that person, to heightened life. The love affair would end (the not-so-young know this), Gladwell Shadrack Chabruma would forget her, she would be elsewhere and forget him, they'd exchange Christmas cards until one or the other moved to a new address, but the farm, the rides alone in the sun and wind with the bony dogs running beside her, the children waving, prancing about, show-ing off, the red earrings of the pepper pods she had seen for the first time; the farm would be one of the experiences knotted into the integument of her life. In development jargon, yes, sus-tainable.

Oh there were times—times she knew when she would crave for this man, a dread distress of anticipation that this would hap-pen. The reserve that characterised him—up-tight, withdrawn—was indeed: a reserve. A reserve of sensuous energy, tenderness and rousing powers of the body. Beneath the armour of the par-liamentary suit there was the passionate assurance, for her, of being desired and—there's another form of capability—the response of desire that revived in her, turned out to be still available from ten, twenty years back. But this coming parting was something other than the expected parting with pleasure. Leaving a country where she had *been before* and where, maybe—she shouldn't indulge herself with the idea—maybe she had made up for the past in some way by her work. Leaving a man; the farm is what she will take away with her from here.

Three months, two months before the tour of duty ends. Meanwhile, something gratifying happened to the Deputy-Director; the Director of Land Affairs was involved in a corruption scandal, and Gladwell Shadrack Chabruma was appointed in his place. She felt a happy, unpossessive pride, on his behalf, another kind of pleasure; the real share in this recognition of his achievements belonged with his family.

Success now changed public reading of his taciturnity, brought the conclusion that it signalled integrity—protected high intelligence, ability, efficiency and *honesty*—he had come clean out of the inquiry that brought the Department into question and caught his superior with, if not a hand in the till, a hand extended to bribes in the granting of land rights to certain individuals and companies, local and international.

One month before the Administrator of the Agency and his Assistant were due to depart; their replacements had arrived, were temporarily accommodated in an hotel; Roberta Blayne was beginning to pack in bubble-wrap the collection of fragile gifts, the clay pots so likely to return, in transit, to the state of their origin, back to handsful of crumbling earth of the country. He came from a parliamentary sub-committee he had chaired, and was telling her about; through the window she saw the driver and bodyguards going off on foot down the drive calling goodbyes to the yard: so he was going to stay the night with her, they were going to make love. He had poured them each a whisky; he was watching her busied with her pots.

She thought she read his scepticism, laughed. —They'll probably be thrown around by the luggage handlers anyway, but I might as well take a chance one or two could survive.—

—I'm going to marry you.—

He said it.

She went on placing a ribbon of sticky tape round the wrapped pot. The tape did not hold and curled back to her fingers.

That is what he said.

He sat down on the sofa where they had been side by side the first time he arrived. *The Deputy-Director is coming to visit you.*

She abandoned the package and came over to him, her fingers entangled in tape, her face a strange grimace of disbelief, amazement, and a loss of control that came out something like a laugh.

He looked at her openly, no need to say it again.

—I'd never be the cause of a divorce. Never. Gladwell. You may not understand that because, well, I know, I've been with you and all along there was your wife. Family. But we both understood. I'd never break up a marriage. Never. It's been good together. I don't have to tell you. I don't know, it wasn't my business to know what . . . the . . . position . . . arrangement is between you and her. In your life. I suppose I was wrong, but I assumed . . . how can I say it . . . we weren't harming her. Oh I'm not such a hypocrite that I don't know you're harming a woman when you sleep with her husband, whether she's aware of it or not, is aware of it and accepts . . . We've been happy—

lucky—anyway I've been—lucky.— She turned and began to unwind the tangle of tape from her fingers, began binding her pot for transport; the gesture was there: *I'm leaving in a month. I'm recalled. You're recalled, my lover, home.* The gesture was a tender and grateful conveyance.

—I am not talking about divorce. She is my wife, of course. Roberta, you will also be my wife. You respect her, I know. She will respect you. It is quite usual in our society. Legal. Always been. We don't have to do what your people do, divorce, remarry, divorce, remarry, and so much trouble and unhappiness, broken homes you're always hearing about. We don't have to follow every custom of the West. You know that. It's what you say in your work. Don't worry. This country, it's now yours, you do real work here you can't do, over there. Good together. I know that, you know that, yes.—

And now she did talk. As bluntly as he did.

She went to the Henderson house on some ordinary pretext and she and Flora chatted pleasantly, desultorily for a while as usual among people with a way of life in common. Then she stopped; as if someone took her by the shoulders, brought her to herself.

—He said he's going to marry me.—

No need to name the lover to this woman friend.

—He's asked you to marry him? Roberta! So it's become really serious? Roberta!—

—Not exactly asked. Said he was going to.—

—Oh well it's just another way of asking, in an affair . . . What'd you say?—

—I would never be the cause of a divorce. Never. But he had no intention . . . — In order to phrase it at a formal distance: —It is to take another wife.—

Flora was smiling, moved by a proposal recognising the qualities of a surrogate marriageable daughter. —You.—

She was conscious of being studied; Flora might never have seen her before. If a love affair changes a woman, as Alan Henderson had privately noticed, the idea of marriage, for a bachelor woman like this one, also brings about a change in the perceptions of a beholder.

—I can't believe it.— Her own voice, empty of expression.

Flora was excitedly intrigued. —But why not. The Minister of Environment and Tourism has two wives and families, I mean it's less common nowadays, they just get divorced instead when they fancy someone else, but it's still accepted. Even part of national pride, for some. There's even talk the President would be happy to do likewise you know—but it wouldn't do to have a meeting with the Queen or the American President with two of them in tow! Why shouldn't the Director of Land Affairs want another wife—a different one. Not necessarily you . . . Why can't you believe it!—

—Not him.—

—You think he's too sophisticated? Our way. But it's obviously because he's serious about you, however you take it, it's a recognition of status, you're not just . . . —

Flora was flattered: for her. At least she had the tact not to ask what the Agency Assistant, bachelor woman, proposed to do next. Was that to be the latest dinner-party story.

Alan, her Administrator, closed the door in his office and he, too, looked at her from yet another perspective than that he had already noted. —Flora's told me about Gladwell. I hope you don't mind.—

—I was going to do so myself, anyway. But we've been so busy since . . . — The Agency was preparing to co-host with the Ministry of Health an international conference on malaria.

—I don't mind admitting to you that Flora and I have talked a lot. She has the idea you are somehow offended by Gladwell.—

It was easier to speak to him than to his wife, there was the trust of their working relationship together.

—No, no, how could I be offended by the idea of being his wife—black man's wife, is that how Flora thinks of it, that's how people would think of it?—when we've been lovers all these months.—

—But Roberta you are offended at the idea of being taken as second wife, you see it as entering some kind of old harem . . . ? So he's offended you, there, no?—

—I can't believe he would ever think of it. That the . . . situation . . . could be a normal part of his life. Now.—

—I'm going to be frank with you. I'm sure he's become very attached to you, but there's another aspect to this—proposal— his wife is a simple woman who takes care of the kids, there's a boy of about ten as well as the grown ones making their way around the world—she shops for the official residence she's so proud of, watches TV; and has nothing to say to him, he obviously can't discuss his work, inside politics and problems of Government, not with her. And you notice she doesn't appear with him at official dinners of the kind when a wife's expected to be along to entertain the wives of visiting bigwigs. You think his idea's a kind of regression, isn't that so. But it's because he needs a companion on his own wave-length at his stage of life and clearly that's what he's found these past months in you. He's seen how astutely you hold your own at meetings, how you can have an—informed—exchange with all kinds of people! That's how he thinks of a second wife. Not a handy bedmate.—

—Alan, you speak as if he's told you all this. But you don't know him that well . . . —

—I don't need to, to know what I've said about his needs— I've my stored profile (touched at his forehead) of men in high public office in developing countries, where women may be beautiful and desirable but social disadvantages, pressures of all kinds—you know them—have deprived them of education, worldliness, if you like. Even now, there aren't enough women here on the level of the Minister of Welfare, that great gal, one of the liveliest MPs, never mind the males . . . And there's something else—strict confidence!—could relate to Gladwell's decision. He's strongly tipped to be made a *Minister* in the President's cabinet reshuffle. So—just that you understand motives. See him from right kind of background perspective we use, you and I—all of us in Agency work. A respect for the others' mores— traditions. Doesn't imply you—we—have to adopt them, of course.—

What Alan Henderson didn't tell her was that in the conclusion of discussion of the startling proposition with his wife, Flora had brought up another perspective on the future cabinet minister's proposal to take Roberta Blayne as number two wife. —She's not the type to go out to attract a man for herself, is she;

this's a chance with a man who's somebody, plenty to offer for a woman like her, she'd have a high position, she loves this country, that farm of his, she'd be able to continue her commitment to development with his influence right up top . . . Not many chances likely to come her way, New York, Geneva . . . Not so young anymore.—

So her colleague the Administrator tacitly understood the rejection she was having to formulate for her lover. She rehearsed to herself in many different, useless ways, how she would have to tell him she couldn't believe he, so completely in charge of himself, a man of the present, free, could want to dredge up into his life some remnant from the past—how could he not have seen that it was offensive, surely to him as to her; how disguise the aversion.

What was the protocol for this.

Then there came to her—Buffalo Mine. How he had received her shame: her taking from him the release of orgasm, blurting the dinner-party story, as if the pleasure were not what her blood-line disqualified her to share, illicit, an orgasm stolen from past betrayal of all that makes up human feeling between people. Every Monday on foot to I. Saretsky every Friday back on foot with the case of whisky head hard as a log. Grandfather's 'my man'; her man, making love to her. He had shown no shock; no revulsion as she blubbered out the shame. He calmed her matter-of-factly, how was it—'It was their tradition'. And now she was primly struggling to conceal how she disdained him for expecting her to accept something he chose from his past; an honour; her ugly past was not his. He absolved her from her burden of ancestry—it's got nothing to do with you: she was in-dicting him for his. It's accepted, Flora said. Their tradition.

Her Administrator had shut the door of his office, once again.
—How's it going?—

—I haven't found a way yet.—

—Look, I can arrange for you to go back ahead of me, re-ports—some such—I want headquarters to evaluate with you before I'm debriefed, you can prepare for me, answering their questions and so on, expanding . . . You could leave right away. Wouldn't that help?—

Of course it would.

The official car arrived. He came to make love with her and it seemed to her the right ending for both of them. He had with-drawn into his old silent self-composure, awaiting her answer without any mention. When they lay together, afterwards, it was the time, coming out of the consolation offered that she still de-sired and received him. —I am going back to New York the day after tomorrow.—

Out of his silence. —You will resign there.—

—No. I have a new posting somewhere.—

She had not found the right words to explain that love affairs are a cul-de-sac on the marriage map. The shining official car concealed in the yard, the royal coach, had turned into a pump-kin. She was again a member of an aid agency's changing per-sonnel, walking away barefoot.

VISITING GEORGE

You remember; we were coming from a conference in that city and I had just noticed we were near the street, the block where the old friends lived. I was thinking—about to say to you—we should drop in, it's been such a long time, we'll be a real surprise, back here again. There were so many people from so many ages; so many periods, approaching us on that London street; in these ancient European cities they are all there in the gait, the shapes of noses and eyes and jowls, the elegant boots and plodding sandals, Shakespeare's audiences, Waterloo's veterans, comportment of the bowler-hatted past, slippered advance of the Oriental counter-immigration from the colonial era, heads of punk-purple-and-green striped hair in recall of 60s Flower Children, androgynous young shuffling in drug daze, icons of the present; black faces that could be the indelible after-image left behind, on the return to Africa by our political exiles. All these, recognisable but not known; coming at us, coming at us. And then he was singled out, for me, they shouldered around him on the pavement but he was directed straight towards us. His paper carrier with the name of a speciality shop, his white curls like suds over thick earlobes—just the way he always was, returning from his pilgrimage to buy mangoes or a bottle of wine from the right slope of a small French vineyard. I saw him.

Wasn't it lovely? Because it *was not* that everything changes. His image was him: the same.

We did go back to that Kensington flat with him? Didn't we? Its watercolours of Tuscan landscapes, engravings of early Cape Town, bold impasto oils by South African black painters he used to discover, music cassettes spilled about, the journals and books to be cleared off the sofa so you could sit. Christ! he said, this old unbeliever, where the hell have you been? People don't write letters any more. We might all have been dead for all we've heard of each other. He railed against whatever conservative government it was (maybe still Thatcher). He, who had left the Party after a visit to the old Soviet Union in the Fifties when he was taken round collective pig farms. But I was thinking—perhaps only thinking now—we all have our point of no return in political loyalty, and the stink of pigs is as good as, say, the disillusion of corruption. He was once detained, back home in the old South Africa, he had paid his dues, earned his entitlement to defect, I suppose, however we might have viewed the pretext.

You don't remember what we talked about? Neither do I. Not really. There he still is, walking out of the weave of people; for us. The apartment: well, as we knew it. But she didn't appear. No. After so long, can one ask . . . ? Maybe asleep, she often said she was an owl, not a lark, liked to lie late. If she's gone—died— or divorced? They've had their contingent loves, that's known. And not only the young have sexual freedom, people find new sexual partners at any age at all. We must wait for him to say something.

But no, he didn't. There are no flowers in the room; she always had majestic vases of blooms and leaves.

So we didn't need any other evidence.

Not there.

But perhaps she was just too busy to buy any flowers that day and he had forgotten her request and gone his usual route to pursue the fresh halibut or the mangoes or the restricted cultivar of a wine?

Will we ever know the significance of apparent trivial forgetfulness, what's ignored, in anyone's life—keys to stages a relationship is passing through. You'll have to invent them. I can't help you. Because I couldn't ask him. Her name didn't come up at all, did it? That close couple, politically involved, risking themselves, never a policy disagreement between them, a stance in total solidarity, together, over the years. Admirable, d'you remember! One commitment, one mind—he always said: we are convinced, we declare ourselves—it was—enviable. Yes.

She didn't have to confirm. No? Ever. Did she?

He forgot the flowers, followed the quest for fish and wine. She's not here, or if she is—

So that's how it always really was. He *made* the opinions, created the 'we', set the itinerary of the political quests. So it didn't—doesn't matter whether she's mentioned or not, does it. *You are, I am, because we have each our opinions. We exist.* Great thought comes to me, eh.

Oh but you do at least remember that we did decide to drop by, having seen him come, known, old friend out of the procession of all the unknown from everywhere who have lived in exile in London. Simply polite to stop by, one forgets old friends too easily. It's a building unaffected by the decline of the borough in this section. Mirrors in the entrance and the old lift behind its screen of wrought-iron scrolls. Number 23, it was on the second floor with the dove-grey door and brass knocker in the form of a graceful hand. It struck the wood discreetly. Their souvenirs from France were more decorative than effective, and as nobody responded, we pressed the bell. Ringing, ringing, questioning through the rooms we knew. It was a woman who opened the door; some woman; not her. The woman heard his name. She said, Mr S——— died four years ago, my husband bought the flat then.

If I dreamt this, while walking, walking in the London streets, the subconscious of each and every other life, past and present, brushing me in passing, what makes it real?

Writing it down.

THE GENERATION GAP

He was the one told: James, the youngest of them. The father to the son—and it was Jamie, with whom he'd never got on since Jamie was a kid; Jamie who ran away when he was adolescent, was brought back resentful, nothing between them but a turned-aside head (the boy's) and the tight tolerant jaw of suppressed disapproval (the father's). Jamie who is doing—what was it now? Running a cybersurfers' restaurant with a friend, that's the latest, he's done so many things but the consensus in the family is that he's the one who's done nothing with his life. His brother and sisters love him but see it as a waste: of charm and some kind of ill-defined talent, sensed but not directed in any of the ways they recognise.

So it was from Jamie that they received the *announcement*. The father had it conveyed by Jamie to them—Virginia, Barbara, and Matthew called at some unearthly hour in Australia. The father has left the mother.

A husband leaves his wife. It is one of the most unexceptional of events. The father has left the mother: that is a completely different version, their version.

A husband leaves his wife for another woman. Of course. Their father, their affectionate, loyal, considerate father, *announces*, just like that: he has left their mother for another woman. Inconceivable.

And to have chosen, of all of them, the younger brother as confidant, confessor, messenger—whatever the reasoning was?

They talked to each other on the telephone, calls those first few days frustratingly blocked while numbers were being dialled simultaneously and the occupied whine sounded on and on. Matthew in Brisbane sent an e-mail. They got together in Barbara's house—his Ba, his favourite. Even Jamie appeared, summoned—for an explanation he could not give.

Why should I ask why, how?

Or would not give. *He* must have said something beyond this announcement; but no. And Jamie had to get back to the bar nook and the espresso machine, leave them to it with his archaic smile of irresponsible comfort in any situation.

And suddenly, from the door—We're all grown up now. Even he.

It was established that no-one had heard from the mother. Ginnie had called her and waited to see if she would say anything, but she chatted about the grandchildren and the progress of a friend she had been visiting in hospital. Not a word. Perhaps she doesn't know. But even if he kept the affair somehow secret from her until now, he would hardly 'inform' his children before telling his wife of a decision to abandon her.

Perhaps she thinks we don't know.

No, can't you see—she doesn't want us to know because she thinks he'll come back, and we don't need ever to know. A private thing. As Jamie said.

That's ridiculous, she's embarrassed, ashamed, I don't know what—humiliated at the idea of us . . .

Ginnie had to intervene as chairperson to restore clarity out of the spurting criss-cross of sibling voices. Now what do we do? What are we talking about: are we going to try and change his mind? Talk some sense into him. Are we going to go to her?

We must. First of all.

Then Ba should go.

One would have thought Ba was the child he would have turned to. She said nothing, stirred in her chair and took a gulp of gin-and-tonic with a pull of lip muscles at its kick. There was no need to ask, why me, because she's her Daddy's favourite, she's closest to him, the one best to understand if anyone can, what has led him to do what he has done—to himself, to their mother.

And the woman? The voices rise as a temperature of the room, what about the woman? Anybody have any idea of who she might be. None of those wives in their circle of friends—it's Alister, Ginnie's husband, considering—Just look at them. Your poor dad.

But where did he and she ever go that he'd meet anyone new? Well, *she'll* know who it is. Ba will be told.

Nothing sure about that.

As the youngest of them said, they're all grown up, there are two among the three present (and that's not counting sports commentator Matthew in Brisbane) who know how affairs may be and are concealed; it's only if they take the place of the marriage that they have to be revealed.

Sick. That's what it is. He's sick.

Ba—all of them anticipating for Ba to deal with the mother—expected tears and heart-break to burst the conventions that protect the intimacy of parents' marriage from their sons and daughters. But there are no tears.

Derision and scorn, from their mother become the discarded wife. Indeed she knows who the woman is. A pause. As if the daughter, not the mother, were the one who must prepare herself.

She's exactly your age, Ba.

And the effect is what the mother must have counted on as part of the kind of triumph she has set herself to make of the disaster, deflecting it to the father. The woman has a child, never been married. Do? Plays the fiddle in an orchestra. How and where he found her, God only knows—you know we never go to concerts, he has his CD collection here in this room. Everything's been just as usual, while it's been going on—he says, very exact—for eight months. So when he finally had the courage to come out with it, I told him, eight months after forty-two years, you've made your choice. May he survive it.

When I said (Ba is reporting), doesn't sound as if it will work for him, it's just an episode, something he's never tried, never done, a missing experience, he'll come back to his life (of course, that would be the way Ba would put it), *she* said—I won't give it back to him. I can't tell you what she's like. It's as if the place they were in together—not just the house—is barricaded. She's in there, guns cocked.

What can they do for her, their mother, who doesn't want sympathy, doesn't want reconciliation brokered even if it were to be possible, doesn't want the healing of their love, any kind of love, if the love of forty-two years doesn't exist.

His Ba offers to bring the three available of his sons and daughters together again to meet him at her house, but he tells her he would rather 'spend some time' with each separately. She is the last he comes to and his presence is strange, both to him and to her. How can it be otherwise? When he sleeps with the woman, she could have been his daughter. It's as if something forbidden has happened between him and his favourite child. Something unspeakable exists.

Ba has already heard it all before—all he will allow himself to tell—from the others. Same story to Ginnie, Jamie and according to an e-mail from Matthew, much the same in a 'bloody awful' call to him. Yes, she is not married, yes, she plays second violin in a symphony orchestra, and yes—she is thirty-five years old. He looks up slowly and he gives his daughter this fact as if he must hold her gaze and she cannot let hers waver; a secret between them. So she feels able to ask him what the others didn't, perhaps because the enquiry might somehow imply acceptance of the validity of happenstance in a preposterous decision of a sixty-seven-year-old to overturn his life. How did he meet this woman?

He shapes that tight tolerant jaw, now not of disapproval (he has no right to that, in these circumstances) but of hurt resignation to probing: on a plane. On a plane! The daughter cannot show her doubtful surprise; when did he ever travel without the mother? While he continues, feeling himself pressed to it: he went to Cape Town for negotiations with principals from the American company who didn't have time to come to him up in Pretoria. The orchestra was going to the coast to open a music festival. He found her beside him. They got talking and she kindly offered to arrange a seat for him at the over-subscribed concert. And then? And then? But her poor father, she couldn't humiliate him, she couldn't follow him, naked, the outer-inner man she'd never seen, through the months in the woman's bed beside the violin case.

What are you going to do, she asked.

It's done.

That's what he said (the siblings compare notes). And he gave such explanation as he could. Practical. I've moved out—but Isabel must have told you. I've taken a furnished flat. I'll leave the number, I'd rather you didn't call at the office, at present.

And then? What will happen to you, my poor father—but all she spoke out was, So you want to marry this girl. For in comparison with his mate, his wife of forty-two years, his sixty-seven years, she is no more than that.

I'll never marry again.

Yes, he told the others that, too. Is the vehemence prudence (the huge age difference, for God's sake: Matthew, from Australia) or is it telling them something about the marriage that produced them, some parental sorrow they weren't aware of while in the family home, or ignored, too preoccupied with their own hived-off lives to bother with, after.

There's nothing wrong between Isabel and me, but for a very long time there's been nothing right, either.

Wishing you every happiness. The wedding gift maxim. Grown apart? Put together mistakenly in the first place—they're all of them too close to the surface marriage created for them, in self-defence and in protection of *them*, the children, no doubt, to be able to speculate.

And what is going to happen to our mother, your Isabel?

And then. And then. That concert, after the indigestion of a three-hour lunch and another three hours of business-speak

wrangling I had with those jocular sharks from Seattle. Mahler's
Symphony No. 1 following Respighi. I've forgotten there's no
comparison between listening to recorded music in a room filled
with all the same things—the photographs, the glass, the coffee
cup in your hand, the chair that fits you—and hearing music,
live. Seeing it, as well, that's the difference, because acoustically
reproduction these days is perfect—I know I used to say it was
better than the bother of driving to concerts. Watching the play-
ers, how they're creating what you're hearing, their movements,
their breathing, the expressions of concentration, even the way
they sit, sway in obedience to the conductor, he's a magician
transforming their bodies into sound. I don't think I took particular notice of her. Maybe I did without knowing it, these things
are a human mystery, I've realised. But that would have been
that—she'd told me her name but I didn't know where she lived,
so I wouldn't even have known where to thank her for the
concert reservation—if it hadn't been that she was on the plane
again next day when I was returning home. We were seated in
the same row, both aisle seats, separated this time only by that
narrow gap we naturally could talk across. About the concert,
what it was like to be a musician, people like myself are always
curious about artists—she was teasing, saying we regard theirs as
a free, undisciplined life compared with being—myself—a businessman, but it was a much more disciplined life than ours—the
rehearsals, the performance, the 'red-eye night-work, endless
overtime' she called it, while we others have regular hours and
leisure. We had the freebie drink together and a sort of mock argument about stress, hers, facing an audience and knowing she'd
get hell afterwards if she played a wrong note, and mine with the
example of the principals from Seattle the day before. The kind

of exchange you hear strangers making on a plane, and that I always avoid.

I avoid now talking about her to my children—what can you call sons and daughters who are far from children. I know they think it's ridiculous—it's all ridiculous, to them—but I don't want anyone running around making 'enquiries' about her, her life, as if her 'suitability' is an issue that has anything to do with them. But of course everything about what I suppose must be called this affair has to do with them because it's their mother, someone they've always seen—will see—as the other half of me. They'll want to put me together again.

The children (he's right, what do you call a couple's grown-up children) often had found weeks go by without meeting one another or getting in touch. Ginnie is a lecturer in the maths department at the university and her husband is a lawyer, their friends are fellow academics and lawyers, with a satisfying link between the two in concerns over the need for a powerful civil society to protect human rights. Their elder son and daughters are almost adult, and they have a late-comer, a four-year-old boy. Ba—she's barren—Ginnie is the repository of this secret of her childlessness. Ba and her husband live in the city as week-long exiles: from the bush. Carl was manager of a wild-life reserve when she fell in love with him, he now manages a branch of clothing chain stores and she is personal secretary to a stockbroker; every weekend they are away, camping and walking, incommunicado to humans, animal-watching, bird-watching, insect-watching, plant-identifying, returned to the lover-arms of the veld. As Ginnie and Alister have remarked, if affectionately, her sister and brother-in-law are more interested in buck and beetles than in any endangered human species. Jamie—to catch up with him, except for Christmas! He was always all over the place other than where you would expect to find him. And Matthew: he was the childhood and adolescence photographs displayed in the parents' house, and a commentator's voice broadcasting a test cricket match from Australia in which recognisable quirks of home pronunciation came and went like the fading and return of an unclear line.

Now they are in touch again as they have not been since a time, times, they wouldn't remember or would remember differently, each according to a need that made this sibling then seek out that, while avoiding the others.

Ginnie and Ba even meet for lunch. It's in a piano bar-cum-bistro with deep armchairs and standing lamps which fan a sunset light to the ceiling beneath which you eat from the low table at your knees. A most unlikely place to be chosen by Ba, who picks at the spicy olives and peri-peri cashew nuts as if she were trying some unfamiliar seed come upon in the wild; but she has suggested the place because she and Carl don't go to restaurants and it's the one she knows of since her stockbroker asks her to make bookings there for him. When the sisters meet they don't know where to begin. The weeks go by, when the phone rings and (fairly regularly, duty bound) it's the father, or (rarely, she's in a mood when duty is seen to be a farce) it's the mother, the siblings have a high moment when it could be another announcement—that it is over, *he's* back, *she's* given his life back to him, the forty-two years. But no, no.

May he survive. That's the axiom the daughters and sons have, ironically, taken from her. Who is this woman who threatens it?

Her name is Alicia (affected choice on the part of whoever engendered her?), surname Parks (commonplace enough, which explains a certain level of origin, perhaps?). She was something of a prodigy for as long as childhood lasts, but has not fulfilled this promise and has ended up no further than second violinist in a second-best symphony orchestra—so rated by people who really know music. Which the father, poor man, doesn't, just his CD shelf in the livingroom, for relaxation with his wife on evenings at home. The woman's career will have impressed him; those who can, play; those who can't, listen: he and Isabel.

What happened to the man, father of the child? Has their father a rival? Is he a hopeful sign? Or—indeed—is he a threat, a complication in the risk the darling crazy sixty-seven-year-old is taking, next thing he'll be mixed up in some *crime passionnel*—but Jamie, captured for drinks at Ginnie's house, laughs—Daddy-O, right on, the older man has appeal! And Jamie's the one who does what as youngsters they called 'picking up stompies'—cigarette butts of information and gossip. The child's father lives in London, he's a journalist and he's said to be a Coloured. So the little boy to whom *he* must be playing surrogate father is a mixed-blood child, twice or thrice diluted, since the father might be heaven knows what concoction of human variety.

At least that shows this business has brought progress in some way. Ginnie is privately returning to something in her own experience of the parental home only one other sibling (Matthew) happens to know about. The parents always affirmed they were not racist and brought up their children that way. So far as they felt they could without conflict with the law of the time. Ginnie, as a student, had a long love affair with a young Indian who was admitted to study at the white university on a quota. She never could tell the parents. When it came to a daughter or son of their own . . .

The fact of the child obviously doesn't matter to *him*, now. Of course the mother, in her present mood, if she gets to hear . . .

Ginnie was at a door of the past, opening contiguous to the present. You never know about anything like that. Principles. Look at me. I wear a ribbon in support of no discrimination against AIDS victims, but what if I found the woman who takes care of my kid was HIV positive—would I get rid of her?

Alister, merely a husband among them, had something to say to the siblings. The matter of the child might be an added attraction for him. The rainbow child. Many well-meaning people in the past now want some way to prove in practice the abstract positions they hid in, then. Of course I don't know your father as well as you do.

His wife had something to add.

Or as we think we do.

Ba did not speak at these family meetings.

She is in a house with her father. The house is something familiar to her but it isn't either the family home or her own. Or maybe it's both—dreams can do these things. Just she and her father; she wonders why he's there in the middle of the day. He says he's waiting for the arrival of the maid. There's the tring-tring of an old-fashioned bicycle bell, the kind they had on their bikes as children. She looks out the window, he's standing behind her, and she sees—they see, she's aware he knows she's looking—a young and pretty redhead/blonde dismount from a bicycle, smiling. But there are no whites who work as maids in this country.

Ginnie and Ba, not telling anyone else, go to a concert. Seats chosen neither too near nor too far back. Yes, she is there with the violin nestling between jaw and shoulder. Follow white hands doing different intricate things, some fingers depressing strings, those of the other hand folded around the bow. She wears the sort of informal evening dress the other women play-ers in the orchestra wear, not quite a uniform; the equivalent of the not quite black-tie outfits the male players allow them-selves—roll-collar shirts and coloured cummerbunds. There's some sort of fringed shawl slipped off the side of the bowing arm. Apparently the dress is quite sexily *décolleté*. They'll verify when the orchestra rises at interval. She is certainly very slim—the left leg stretched gracefully, and there's a lot of hair piled on top of her head. Not blonde, not redhead. It's the colour of every second woman's at present, an unidentifiable brown overlaid with a purplish shine of henna. She rests her bow, plays when summoned by the conductor, and the sisters are summoned to listen to her. They feel she knows they are there, although she doesn't know them. She's looking at them although blinded by the stage lights. She's playing to *them*.

The palm of the hand.

All that you go through your life (sixty-seven years, how long it's been) without knowing. Most of it you'll never suspect you lack and it's pure chance that you may come upon. An ordinary short flight between one familiar city and another in daily, yearly time. The palm of a hand: that it can be so erotic. Its pads and valleys and lines to trace and kiss; she laughs at me and says they're lines of fortune, that's why I'm here with her. The palm that holds enfolds the rod of the bow and it sings. Enfolds holds me.

Matthew mustn't think he can stay out of it! They send him e-mail letters, despatched by Ginnie but addressing him as from a collective 'we'—the sisters and their husbands, the younger brother—who expect him to take part in decisions: whatever there is to be done. Matthew writes, I suppose we gave them the general amount of trouble sons and daughters do. The parents, he means. And what is meant by that? What's that got to do with anything that can be done? What's he getting at? Is it that it's the parents' turn now—for God's sake, at their, at *his* age! Or is it that because of their past youth the sons and daughters ought to understand the parents better? All these irrelevances—relevances, who knows—come upon, brought up by the one nice and far-away among the cricket bats and kangaroos. What is there for Matthew to disinter; he was always so uncomplicated—so far as they know, those who grew up close to him in the entanglements of a family; never ran away from anything—unless you count Australia, where he's made what is widely recognised as a success.

The general amount of trouble. Jamie. And for the parents he's unlikely ever to be regarded as anything other than troubling. *As long as they're happy*, parents say of their engendered adults, swallowing dismay and disappointment. What did the parents really know of what was happening to their young, back then. Ginnie's Indian; the irony, she sees it now, that it was his parents who found out about the affair and broke it off. Never mind falling in love, that kind of love was called miscegenation in those days, punishable by law, and would have put his studies at risk; his parents planned for him to be a doctor, not a lover—in prison. Ba's abortion. How *he* would have anguished over his favourite daughter if he had known. Only Ginnie knows that this botched back-room process is the reason why Ba is childless. No-one else; not Carl. It belongs to a life before Ba found him, her rare and only elect mate, come upon in the bush. It's unlikely that Jamie has a passing thought (in the reminder of the general amount of trouble they've given) for what he arranged for his frantic sister, that time; even as a teenager he had precociously the kind of friends who were used to mutual efforts in getting one another out of all manner of youthful trouble. Yes, it was Jamie—Jamie of all of them—Ba turned to; as it was Jamie—of all of them—her father had turned to in his trouble, now.

It became possible to have *him* to eat a meal at one or other of their homes, without the mother. As if it were normal. And not easy to convey to him implicitly that it was not; that his place as a lover was not at this table, his place here was as a husband with his wife, mother-and-father. This displacement did not apply to their mother because she, as they saw it, was the victim of this invading lover in the family circle. She had accepted to come to them, in her own right (so to speak), now and then, her carefully erected composure forbidding any discussion of the situation at table, and now she had gone to spend a holiday with her cousin, a consular official in Mauritius.

After the meal with her at Ginnie's or Ba's house, one of them, her daughters or their husbands, insisted on a sense of reality by bringing up the subject; the only subject. How did things stand now? Was there any exchange of ideas, say, about the future, going on between *him* and her?

Her lawyer had met him and an allowance for her had been arranged; there were other matters to be cleared up. Possessions. These were not specified, as if it had nothing to do with anyone but herself. It was Carl who was able to say, out of his privileged innocence close to nature's organic cycles of change and renewal, Maybe your absence will be the right thing. For both of you. When you come back you may find you can work things out again together.

She looked at him half-pityingly, for his concern.

Things are worked out. It was his work.

And she turned away *as of her right* to grandmotherly talk with Ginnie's small boy, for whom she had brought a model jeep, and then to a low exchange in intimate tone with her favourite, the elder of the two teenage daughters, who happened to be at home in the family that evening. No boyfriends around tonight? Usually when I come at the weekend I hear a lot of music and laughing going on upstairs. Helen's friends, the girl says. And not yours, not your type—I understand. What's your type . . . all right, *the* one, then—I have a pretty good idea of what would interest you, you know.

And the girl lies, describing the non-existent one as she thinks an adult would wish him to be.

When the mother-grandmother had left, Ginnie's husband Alister told them: Isabel thinks we're on *his* side, that's the problem.

Why should we be. —Nobody takes up Ba's statement.

May he survive.

Best of all. Early in the morning some days to wake at the sound of the key turning in the lock; her key. Hear it but not sufficiently awake to open eyes; and there's a cold fresh cheek laid against the unshaven one. She's left her apartment before seven to deliver the child to nursery school and after, she's suddenly here. Yesterday. Heard her shoes drop and opened eyes to follow her clothes to the floor. She glides into bed, the cheek is still cold and the rest of her is her special warmth. Not today: waiting for the key to turn. Tomorrow. Again it will turn. Again and again.

They broach to one another the obligation—the usefulness, perhaps—of inviting him to bring her along some time. Sunday lunch? No, too familiar a gesture, and Ba and Carl would not be there, why should Ginnie and Alister deal with this on their own, you can't count on Jamie. Come by for a drink sixish, that would do. What's she like—look like? The two men want to know in advance—after all, they are the father's fellow males—what to expect in order to put themselves in his place. But the splash of stage lights drops a mask on faces, there were cave-hollows of eyes, white cheeks, bright mouth. It was the hands in movement by which an identity was followed.

The man who brings her to Ginnie's house is another personage: their father? He who always listened, talks. Although this is not his home, he is not the host, he rises to refill glasses and offer snacks. He is courting her, in front of them, they see it! Their mother is much better-looking; still beautiful; this one has a long, thin, voracious face, the light did not exaggerate its hollows, and her intelligently narrowed eyes—hazel? greenish? doesn't matter—are iconised by makeup in the style of Egyptian statues. She's chosen a loose but clinging tunic and the sisters see that she has firm breasts. When they compare impressions afterwards it seems it was the women who noted this rather than, as they would have thought, the men. Her hands are unadorned (the mother has had gifts of beautiful rings from *him*, over the years) and lie half-curled, the palms half-open on chair-arm or lap; it's as if the hands' lack of tension is meant to put them at ease, these hands that make music. And pleasure their father. She has a voice with what the women suspect as an adopted huskiness they believe men find attractive. It turns out no-one of the men—Jamie was present—noticed it either as an affectation or an attraction *he* might have responded to.

The talk was quite animated and completely artificial; they were *all* other people; chatting about nothing that mattered to whom and what they really were. There are so many harmless subjects, you can really get along in any situation by sticking to what has been in the newspapers and on television about the floods/drought, the times of day to avoid driving in traffic congestion (keep off wars and politics, both local and international, those are intimate subjects), and, of course about music. It is the lover who brings that up; Ginnie and Ba would have preferred to keep off that, too. She might somehow sense how their eyes had been upon her while she played . . . *He* even boasts about her: Alicia will go with the orchestra to an international music festival in Montreal in the winter, and it will be particularly enjoyable for her because Alicia also speaks fluent French. He might be—ought to be—boring someone with the achievements of his seventeen-year-old grand-daughter, Ginnie's eldest child. Ginnie's biological after-thought, four-year-old Shaun, had been playing with his jeep around everyone's feet. When the father and his woman were leaving, she bent to the child: I've got a little boy like you, you know. He has a collection of cars but I don't think he has a jeep, yours's great.

They are not embarrassed about anything, these lovers.

The new father of some other man's progeny makes a pledge for the rainbow child. We'll have to find one for him. Where did you get it?

Shaun asserts the presence not admitted to the drinks party. My grandmother did bring it for me.

A curious—almost shaming—moment comes to the siblings and husbands when they suddenly laugh about the whole business—mother, father, the woman. It begins to happen when they get together—less and less frequently—dutifully to try and decide yet again what they ought to be doing about it. The outbreak's akin to the hysterical giggle that sometimes accompanies tearful frustration. What can you do about Papa in his bemused state, and oh my God, next thing is he'll get her pregnant, he'll be Daddy all over again. No no no—spare us that! What do you mean *no*—presumably that's what it's all about, his pride in an old man's intact male prowess! And Alister in an aside to Jamie—Apparently he's still able to get it up—right on, as you would say—and they all lose control again. What is there to do with the mother who is unapproachable, wants to be left alone like a sulky teenager, and a father who's broken loose like a youth sowing wild oats? Who could ever do anything with people in such conditions? Ah—but these are mature people! So nobody knows what maturity is, after all? Is that it? Not any longer, not any more, now that the mother and father have taken away that certainty from their sons and daughters. Matthew calls and sends e-mail from his safe distance, reproaching, What is the matter with all of you? Why can't you get some reality into them, bring them together for what's left after their forty-two years? How else can this end?

Well, the mother seems to be making an extended holiday-of-a-lifetime out of the situation, and *he*, he's out of reach (spaced out: Jamie) dancing to a fiddle. Shaking their heads with laughter; that dies in exasperation. There's *nothing* you can do with the parents.

Only fear for them. Ba's tears are not of laughter.

At least adolescents grow up; that could have been counted on to solve most of the general trouble they'd given. In the circumstances of parents it seems there isn't anything to be counted on, least of all the much-vaunted wisdom of old age. The mother wrote a long round-robin letter (copy to each sibling, just a different name after 'Dearest') telling that she was going to Matthew in Australia. So Mauritius had been halfway there, halfway from her rightful home, all along, in more than its geographical position across the Indian Ocean between Africa and Australia. She would 'keep house' in Matthew's bachelor apartment while she looked for a new place of her own, with space enough for them to come and visit her. Send the grandchildren.

Alicia Parks, second violinist, did not return from Montreal. *He* continued to exchange letters and calls with her over many months. The family gathered this when he gave them news of her successes with the orchestra on tour, as if whether this was of interest or welcome to them or not, they must recognise her as an extension of his life—and therefore theirs. They, it obviously implied, could make up their minds about that.

What he did not tell them was that she had left the orchestra at the invitation to join a Montreal chamber group. As first violinist: an ambition he knew she had and he wanted to see fulfilled for her. But Canada. She had taken into consideration (that was her phrase) that there were not many such opportunities for her back in Africa.

With him. In his long late-night calls to her he completed, to himself, what she didn't say.

She sent for her child; told him only after the child had left the country. Then she did not tell him that she was with someone other than her child, a new man, but he knew from her voice.

Ginnie came out with it to their father. Is she coming back?

When she gets suitable engagements here, of course. She's made a position for herself in the world of music.

So he's waiting for her, they decided, poor man. Why can't he accept it's over, inevitably, put the whole thing behind him, come back to ageing as a *father*, there's a dignified alternative to this disastrous regression to adolescence.

May he survive.

Together and individually, they are determined in pursuit of him.

The best was the cold cheek. Just that. What alternative to that.

In the mirror in the bathroom, there was her body as she dried herself after the love-making bath together, towelling between her spread legs, and then across the back of her neck as beautifully as she bowed across the violin, steam sending trickles of her hair over her forehead. A mirror full of her. For me, old lover she knew how to love so well, so well, her old lover sixty-seven. What alternative.

Death is a blank mirror, emptied of all it has seen and shown.

Death waits, was waiting, but I took the plane to Cape Town, instead.

L, U, C, I, E.

My name's Lucie—no, not with a 'y'. I've been correcting that all my life, ever since my name was no longer vocables I heard and responded to like a little domestic animal (here, puss, puss) and I learnt to draw these tones and half-tones as a series of outlines: L,U,C,I,E. This insistence has nothing to do with identity. The so-called search for identity bores me. I know who I am. You know well enough who you are: every ridge in a toe-nail, every thought you keep private, every opinion you express is your form of life and your responsibility. I correct the spelling because I'm a lawyer and I'm accustomed to precision in language; in legal documents the displacement of a comma can change the intention expressed in a sentence and lead to new litigation. It's a habit, my pedantry; as a matter of fact, in this instance simply perpetuates another orthographic inaccuracy: I'm named for my father's Italian grandmother, and the correct Italian form of the name is Lucia. This had no significance for me until I saw her name on her tomb: LUCIE.

I've just been on holiday in Italy with my father. My mother died a few months ago; it was one of those journeys taken after the death of a wife when the male who has survived sees the daughter as the clone woman who, taken out of present time and place to the past and another country, will protect him from the proximity of death and restore him to the domain of life. (I only hope my father has understood that this was one-off, temporary, a gift from me.) I let him believe it was the other way round: he was restoring something to me by taking me to the village where, for him, I had my origin. He spent the first five years of his life dumped by poor parents in the care of that grandmother, and although he then emigrated to Africa with them and never returned, his attachment to her seems never to have been replaced. By his mother, or anyone else; long after, hers was the name he gave to his daughter.

He has been to Europe so many times—with my mother, almost every year.

'Why haven't you come here before?' I asked him. We were sitting in a sloping meadow on what used to be the family farm of his grandmother and her maiden sisters. The old farmhouse where he spent the years the Jesuits believe definitive had been sold, renovated with the pink and green terrace tiles, curly-cue iron railings and urns of red geraniums favoured by successful artisans from the new industrial development that had come up close to the village. The house was behind us; we could forget it, he could forget its usurpation. A mulberry tree shaded the meadow like a straw hat. As the sun moved, so did the cast of its brim. He didn't answer; a sudden volley of shooting did—stuttering back and forth from the hills in cracking echoes through the peace where my question drifted with the evaporating moisture of grass.

The army had a shooting range up there hidden in the chestnut forests, that was all; like a passing plane rucking the fabric of perfect silence, the shots brought all that shatters continuity in life, the violence of emotions, the trajectories of demands and

contests of will. My mother wanted to go to art galleries and theatres in great European cities, he was gratified to be invited to
speak at conferences in Hong Kong and Toronto, there were
wars and the private wars of cartels and, for all I know, love affairs—all that kept him away. He held this self hidden from me,
as parents do in order to retain what they consider a suitable image before their children. Now he wanted to let me into his life,
to confirm it, as if I had been a familiar all along.

We stayed in the only albergo in the village and ate our meals
in a dark bar beneath the mounted heads of stag and mountain
goats. The mother of the proprietor was brought to see my father, whom she claimed to remember as a small child. She snif-
fled, of course, recollecting the three sisters who were the last of
a family who had been part of the village so long that—that
what? My father was translating for me, but hesitantly, not much
is left of his Italian. So long that his grandmother's mother had
bred silkworms, feeding them on mulberry leaves from her own
trees, and spinning silk as part of the home industry which existed in the region before silk from the Orient took away the
market. The church square where he vividly remembered playing was still there and the nuns still ran an infant school where
he thought he might have been enrolled for a few months. Perhaps he was unhappy at the school and so now could not picture
himself entering that blue door, before us where we sat on a
bench beside the church. The energy of roaring motorcycles carrying young workers in brilliantly studded and sequinned wind-
breakers to the footwear and automobile parts factories ripped
his voice away as he told me of the games drawn with a stick in
the dust, the cold bliss of kicking snow about, and the hot flat
bread sprinkled with oil and salt the children would eat as a

morning snack. Somewhere buried in him was a blue-pearl, translucent light of candles that distorted 'like water' he said, some figures that were not real people. In the church, whose bells rang the hours tremulously from hill to hill, there were only the scratched tracings of effaced murals; he thought the image must have come from some great event in his babyhood, probably the local saint's day visit to a shrine in a neighbouring town.

We drove there and entered the chapels along the sides of a huge airport-concourse of a basilica—my mother was not a Catholic and this analogy comes to me naturally out of my experience only of secular spaces. There were cruel and mournful oil paintings behind the liquid gouts of votive candlelight; he dropped some coins in the box provided but did not take a candle, I don't know whether the dingy representation of the present snuffed out his radiant image or whether his image transformed it for him. We had strong coffee and cakes named for the shrine, in an arcade of delicious-smelling cafés opposite. He had not tasted those cakes for fifty-eight years, since Lucie bought them as a treat; we had found the right context for the candles that had kept alight inside him all that time. The cafés were filled with voluble old men, arguing and gesticulating with evident pleasure. They were darkly unshaven and wore snappy hats. I said: 'If you'd stayed, you'd be one of them' and I didn't know whether I'd meant it maliciously or because I was beguiled by the breath of vanilla and coffee into the fascination of those who have a past to discover.

At night he drank grappa in the bar with the proprietor and picked up what he could of the arguments of village cronies and young bloods over the merits of football teams, while the TV babbled on as an ignored attraction. These grandchildren of the patriarchs blew in on a splendid gust created by the sudden arrest of speed as they cut the engines of their motorcycles. They disarrayed themselves, flourishing aside tinsel-enamelled or purple-luminous helmets and shaking out haloes of stiff curls and falls of blond-streaked locks. They teased the old men, who seemed to tolerate this indulgently, grinningly, as a nostalgic resurrection of their own, if different, wild days.

No women came to the bar. Up in my room each night, I leant out of my window before bed; I didn't know how long I stayed like that, glitteringly bathed in the vast mist that drowned the entire valley between the window and the dark rope of the Alps' foothills from which it was suspended, until the church clock—a gong struck—sent waves layering through the mist that I had the impression I could see undulating silvery, but which I was feeling, instead, reverberating through my rib-cage. There was nothing to see, nothing. Yet there was the tingling perception, neither aural nor visual, that overwhelms in the swoon before an anaesthetic whips away consciousness. The night before we went to the cemetery, I was quite drunk with it. The reflection of the moon seeped through the endless insubstantial surface, silence inundated this place he had brought me to; the village existed out there no more than it had ever done for me when I had never sat in its square, never eaten under the glass eyes of timid beasts killed in its chestnut forests and mountains, or sat in the shade of its surviving mulberry tree.

We had four days. On our last afternoon, he said 'Let's walk up to the old cemetery.' My mother was cremated—so there was no question of returning painfully to the kind of scene where we had parted with her; still, I should have thought in his mood death was too close to him for him to have found it easy to approach any of its territory. But it seemed this was just one of the directions we hadn't yet taken on the walks where he had shown me what he believed belonged to me, given in naming me.

We wandered up to this landmark as we had to others. He took a wrong turning into a lane where there were plaster gnomes and a miniature windmill on a terrace, and canaries sang for their caged lives, piercingly as cicadas. But he retraced our steps and found the right cartographical signals of memory. There was a palatial iron gateway surmounted by a cross, and beyond walls powdery with saltpetre and patched with moss, the black forefingers of cypress trees pointed. Inside: a vacuum, no breath, flowers in green water, withered.

I had never seen a cemetery like that; tombs, yes, and elaborate tableaux of angels over grave-stones—but here, in addition to a maze of these there were shelves and shelves of stone-faced compartments along the inner side of the walls, each with its plaque.

Were the dead stored, filed away?

'When there's no room left for graves, it's usual in this country. Or maybe it's just cheaper.' But he was looking for something.

'They're all here' he said. We stepped carefully on gravelled alleys between tombstones and there they were, uncles and aunts and sons and daughters, cousins who had not survived infancy and other collaterals who had lived almost a century, lived through the collapse of the silkworm industry, the departures of their grown children to find an unknown called a better life in other countries, lived on through foreign occupation during a war and through the coming of the footwear and automobile parts factories—all looking out from photographs framed under convex glass and fixed to their tombstones. No face was old, or sick, or worn. Whenever it was they had died, here they consorted in the aspect they had had when young or vigorously mature.

There were many Albertos and Giovannis and Marias and Clementinas, but the names most honoured by being passed on were Carlo and Lucia, apparently those of the first progenitors to be recorded. Five or six Lucias, from a child in ringlets to fat matrons inclining their heads towards their husbands, many of whom were buried beside them; and then we came to—he came to—her grave. Her sisters were on either side of her. I couldn't read the rest of the inscription, but LUCIE was incised into the ice-smooth black marble. I leant to look. Go on, he said, giving me the example of bracing his foot on the block that covered her. Under her oval bubble of glass the woman was composed and smooth-haired, with the pupil-less gaze of black eyes, the slightly distended nostrils and straight mouth with indented corners of strong will, and the long neck, emphasized by tear-drop earrings, of Italian beauties. Her eyebrows were too thick; if she had belonged to another generation she would have plucked them and spoiled her looks. He put his arm on my shoulder. 'There's a resemblance.' I shrugged it off with his hand. If your name is on your tombstone, it's definitive, it's not some casual misspelling. Why wasn't she Lucia, like the others?

'I don't really know—only what I was told by my father, and he didn't say much . . . parents in those days . . . the sisters kept their mouths shut, I suppose, and in any case he was away working at the docks in Nice from the age of eighteen . . . Apparently she had also gone to work in France when she was very young— the family was poor, no opportunity here. She was a maid in an hotel, and there's something about her having had a love affair with a Frenchman who used the French version of her name . . . and so she kept it, even when she married my grandfather.'

While he was talking a dust-breeze had come up, sweeping its broom among the graves, stirring something that made me tighten my nostrils. The smell of slimy water in the vases of shrivelled flowers and the curious stagnant atmosphere of a walled and crowded space where no living person breathed— what I had taken in when we entered the place was strengthened by some sort of sweetness. With his left foot intimately weighted against her grave, the way a child leans against the knee of a loved adult, he was still talking: 'There's the other version—it comes from *her* mother, that it was *her mother* who was a maid in Nice and my grandmother was her illegitimate child.' I was looking at the foot in the pump-soled running shoe, one of the pair he had kitted himself out with at the market in Cuneo on our way to the village. 'She brought the baby home, and all that remained of the affair was the spelling of the name.' Dust blew into my eyes, the cloying sweetness caught in my throat and coated my tongue. I wanted to spit. '. . . what the maiden sisters thought of that, how she held out against them? God knows . . . I don't remember any man in the house, I would have remembered . . .'

The sweetness was sickly, growing like some thick liquor loading the air. We both inhaled it, it showed in the controlled grimace that wrinkled round his eyes and mouth and I felt the same reaction pulling at my own face muscles. But he went on talking, between pauses; in them we neither of us said anything about the smell, the smell, the smell like that of a chicken gone

bad at the back of a refrigerator, a rat poisoned behind a wain-
scot, a run-over dog swollen at a roadside, the stench, stench of
rotting flesh, and all the perfumes of the living body, the clean
salty tears and saliva, the thrilling fluids of love-making, the
scent of warm hair, turned putrid. Unbearable fermentation of
the sweetness of life. It couldn't have been her. It could not have
been coming to him from her, she had been dead so long, but he
stayed there with his foot on her stone as if he had to show me
that there was no stink in our noses, as if he had to convince
me that it wasn't her legacy.

We left saunteringly ignoring the gusts of foulness that
pressed against us, each secretly taking only shallow breaths in
revulsion from the past. At the gate we met a woman in the
backless slippers and flowered overall local women wore everywhere except to go to church. She saw on our faces what was expressed in hers, but hers was mixed with some sort of apologetic
shame and distress. She spoke to him and he said something reassuring, using his hands and shaking his head. She repeated
what she had told him and began to enlarge on it; I stood by,
holding my breath as long as I could. We had some difficulty in
getting away from her, out beyond the walls where we could
stride and breathe.

'A young man was killed on his motorbike last week.'

What was there to say?

'I didn't see a new grave.'

'No—he's in one of the shelves—that's why . . . She says it
takes some time, in there.'

So it wasn't the secrets of the rotting past, Lucie's secrets, it
was the secret of the present, always present; the present was just

as much there, in that walled place of the dead, as it was where the young bloods, like that one, tossed down their bright helmets in the bar, raced towards death, like that one, scattering admiring children in the church square.

Now when I write my name, that is what I understand by it.

LOOK-ALIKES

It was scarcely worth noticing at first; an out-of-work lying under one of the rare indigenous shrubs cultivated by the Botany Department on campus. Some of us remembered, afterwards, having passed him. And he—or another like him—was seen rummaging in the refuse bins behind the Student Union; one of us (a girl, of course) thrust out awkwardly to him a pitta she'd just bought for herself at the canteen, and she flushed with humiliation as he turned away mumbling. When there were more of them, the woman in charge of catering came out with a kitchen-hand in a blood-streaked apron to chase them off like a band of marauding monkeys.

We were accustomed to seeing them pan-handling in the streets of the city near the university and gathered in this vacant lot or that, clandestine with only one secret mission, to beg enough to buy another bottle; moving on as the druids' circle of their boxes and bits of board spread on the ground round the ashes of their trash fires was cleared for the erection of post-modern office blocks. We all knew the one who waved cars into empty parking bays. We'd all been confronted, as we crossed the road or waited at the traffic lights, idling in our minds as the en-gine of the jalopy idles, by the one who held up a piece of cardboard with a message running out of space at the edges: NO JOB IM HUNGRY EVEYONE HELP PLeas.

At first; yes, there were already a few of them about. They must have drifted in by the old, unfrequented entrance down near the tennis courts, where the security fence was not yet completed. And if they were not come upon, there were the signs: trampled spaces in the bushes, empty bottles, a single split shoe with a sole like a lolling tongue. No doubt they had been chased out by a patrolling security guard. No student, at that stage, would have bothered to report the harmless presence; those of us who had cars might have been more careful than usual to leave no sweaters or radios visible through the locked windows. We followed our familiar rabbit-runs from the lecture rooms and laboratories back, forth and around campus, between residences, libraries, Student Union and swimming pool, through avenues of posters making announcements of debates and sports events, discos and rap sessions, the meetings of Muslim, Christian or Jewish brotherhoods, gay or feminist sisterhoods, with the same lack of attention to all but the ones we'd put up ourselves.

It was summer when it all started. We spend a lot of time on the lawns around the pool, in summer. We swot down there, we get a good preview of each other more or less nude, boys and girls, there's plenty of what you might call foreplay—happy necking. And the water to cool off in. The serious competitive swimmers come early in the morning when nobody else is up, and it was they who discovered these people washing clothes in the pool. When the swimmers warned them off they laughed and jeered. One left a dirt-stiff pair of pants that a swimmer balled and threw after him. There was argument among the swimmers; one felt the incident ought to be reported to Security, two were uncomfortable with the idea in view of the university's commitment to being available to the city community. They must have persuaded him that he would be exposed for elitism, because although the pool was referred to as The Wishee-Washee, among us, after that, there seemed to be no action taken.

Now you began to see them all over. Some greeted you smarmily (*my baas*, sir, according to their colour and culture), retreating humbly into the undergrowth, others, bold on wine or stoned on meths, sentimental on pot, or transformed in the wild hubris of all three, called out a claim (Hey man, *Ja boetie*) and even beckoned to you to join them where they had formed one of their circles, or huddled, just two, with the instinct for seclusion that only couples looking for a place to make love have, among us. The security fence down at the tennis courts was completed, reinforced with spikes and manned guard-house, but somehow they got in. The guards with their Alsatian dogs patrolled the campus at night but every day there were more shambling figures disappearing into the trees, more of those thick and battered faces looking up from the wells between buildings, more supine bodies contoured like sacks of grass-cuttings against the earth beneath the struts of the sports grandstands.

And they were no longer a silent presence. Their laughter and their quarrels broadcast over our student discussions, our tête-à-tête conversations and love-making, even our raucous fooling about. They had made a kind of encampment for themselves, there behind the sports fields where there was a stretch of ground whose use the university had not yet determined: it was for future expansion of some kind, and in the meantime equipment for maintenance of the campus was kept there—objects that might or might not be useful, an old tractor, barrels for indoor plants when the Vice-Chancellor requested a bower to decorate some hall for the reception of distinguished guests, and—of course—the compost heaps. The compost heaps were now being used as a repository for more than garden waste. If they had not been there with their odours of rot sharpened by the chemical agents for decay with which they were treated, the conclave living down there might have been sniffed out sooner. Perhaps they had calculated this in the secrets of living rough: perhaps they decided that the Alsatians' noses would be bamboozled.

So we knew about them—everybody knew about them, students, faculty, administrative staff, Vice-Chancellor—and yet nobody knew about them. Not officially. Security was supposed to deal with trespassers as a routine duty; but although Security was able to find and escort beyond the gates one or two individuals too befuddled or not wily enough to keep out of the way, they came back or were replaced by others. There was some kind of accommodation they had worked out within the order of the campus, some plan of interstices they had that the university didn't have; like the hours at which security patrols could be expected, there must have been other certainties we students and our learned teachers had relied on so long we did not realize that they had become useless as those red bomb-shaped fire extinguishers which, when a fire leaps out in a room, are found to have evaporated their content while hanging on the wall.

We came to recognise some of the bolder characters; or rather it was that they got to recognise us—with their street-wise judgment they knew who could be approached. For a cigarette. Not money—you obviously don't ask students for what they themselves are always short of. They would point to a wrist and ask the time, as an opener. And they must have recognised something else, too; those among us who come to a university because it's the cover where you think you can be safe from surveillance and the expectations others have of you—back to play-school days, only the sand-pit and the finger-painting are substituted by other games. The dropouts, just cruising along until the end of the academic year, sometimes joined the group down behind the grandstands, taking a turn with the zol and maybe helping out with the donation of a bottle of wine now and then. Of course only we, their siblings, identified them; with their jeans bought ready-torn at the knees, and hair shaved up to a topknot, they would not have been distinguished from the younger men in the group by a passing professor dismayed at the sight of the intrusion of the campus by hobos and loafers. (An interesting point, for the English Department, that in popular terminology the whites are known as hobos and the blacks as loafers.) If student solidarity with the underdog was expressed in the wearing of ragged clothes, then the invaders' claim to be within society was made through adoption of acceptable fashionable unconventions. (I thought of putting that in my next essay for Sociology II.) There were topknots and single earrings among the younger invaders, dreadlocks, and one had long tangled blond hair snaking about his dark-stubbled face. He could even have passed for a certain junior lecturer in the Department of Political Science.

So nobody said a word about these recruits from among the students, down there. Not even the Society of Christian Students, who campaigned for moral regeneration on the campus. In the meantime, 'the general situation had been brought to the notice' of Administration. The implication was that the intruders were to be requested to leave, with semantic evasion of the terms 'squatter' or 'eviction'. SUJUS (Students For Justice) held a meeting in protest against forced removal under any euphemism. ASOCS (Association of Conservative Students) sent a delegation to the Vice-Chancellor to demand that the campus be cleared of degenerates.

Then it was discovered that there were several women living among the men down there. The white woman was the familiar one who worked along the cars parked in the streets, trudging in thonged rubber sandals on swollen feet. The faces of the two black women were darkened by drink as white faces are reddened by it. The three women were seen swaying together, keeping upright on the principle of a tripod. The Feminist Forum took them food, tampons, and condoms for their protection against pregnancy and AIDS, although it was difficult to judge which was still young enough to be a sex object in need of protection; they might be merely prematurely aged by the engorged tissues puffing up their faces and the exposure of their skin to all weathers, just as, in a reverse process, pampered females look younger than they are through the effect of potions and plastic surgery.

From ASOCS came the rumour that one of the group had made obscene advances to a girl student—although she denied this in tears, *she* had offered *him* her pitta, which he had refused, mumbling 'I don't eat rubbish'. The Vice-Chancellor was importuned by parents who objected to their sons' and daughters' exposure to undesirables, and by Hope For The Homeless who wanted to put up tents on this territory of the over-privileged. The City Health authorities were driven off the campus by SUJUS and The Feminist Forum while the Jewish Student Congress discussed getting the Medical School to open a clinic down at the grandstands, the Islamic Student Association took a collection for the group while declaring that the area of their occupation was out of bounds to female students wearing the *chador*, and the Students Buddhist Society distributed tracts on meditation among men and women quietly sleeping in the sun with their half-jacks, discreet in brown paper packets up to the screw-top, snug beside them as hot-water bottles.

These people could have been removed by the police, of course, on a charge of vagrancy or some such, but the Vice-Chancellor, the University Council, and the Faculty Association had had too much experience of violence resulting from the presence of the police on campus to invite this again. The matter was referred back and forth. When we students returned after the Easter vacation the blond man known by his head of hair, the toothless ones, the black woman who always called out *Hullo lovey how'you* and the neat queen who would buttonhole anyone to tell of his student days in Dublin, *You kids don't know what a real university is*, were still there. Like the stray cats students (girls again) stooped to scratch behind the ears.

And then something really happened. One afternoon I thought I saw Professor Jepson in a little huddle of four or five comfortably under a tree on their fruit-box seats. Someone who looked the image of him; one of the older men, having been around the campus some months, now, was taking on some form of mimesis better suited to him than the kid-stuff garb the younger ones and the students aped from each other. Then I saw him again, and there was Dr Heimrath from Philosophy just in the act of taking a draw, next to him—if any social reject wanted a model for look-alike it would be from that Department. And I was not alone, either; the friend I was with that day saw what I did. We were the only ones who believed a student who said he had almost stepped on Bell, Senior Lecturer from Math, in the bushes with one of the three women; Bell's bald head shone a warning signal just in time. Others said they'd seen Kort wrangling with one of the men, there were always fights when the gatherings ran out of wine and went onto meths. Of course Kort had every kind of pure alcohol available to him in his domain, the science laboratories; everybody saw him, again and again, down there, it was Kort, all right, no chance of simple resemblance, and the euphoria followed by aggression that a meths concoction produces markedly increased in the open-air coterie during the following weeks. The papers Math students handed in were not returned when they were due; Bell's secretary did not connect calls to his office, day after day, telling callers he had stepped out for a moment. Jepson, Professor Jepson who not only had an international reputation as a nuclear physicist but also was revered by the student body as the one member of faculty who was always to be trusted to defend students' rights against authoritarianism, our old prof, everybody's enlightened grandfather—he walked down a corridor unbuttoned, stained, with dilated pupils that were unaware of the students who shrank back, silent, to make way.

There had been sniggers and jokes about the other faculty members, but nobody found anything to say over Professor Jepson; nothing, nothing at all. As if to smother any comment about him, rumours about others got wilder; or facts did. It was said that the Vice-Chancellor himself was seen down there, sitting round one of their trash fires; but it could have been that he was there to reason with the trespassers, to flatter them with the respect of placing himself in their company so that he could deal with the situation. Heimrath was supposed to have been with him, and Bester from Religious Studies with Franklin-Turner from English—but Franklin-Turner was hanging around there a lot, anyway, that snobbish closet drinker come out into the cold, no more fastidious ideas about race keeping him out of that mixed company, eh?

And it was no rumour that Professor Russo was going down there, now. Minerva Russo, of Classics, young, untouchable as one of those lovely creatures who can't be possessed by men, can be carried off only by a bull or penetrated only by the snowy penis-neck of a swan. We males all had understood, through her, what it means to feast with your eyes, but we never speculated about what we'd find under her clothes; further sexual awe, perhaps, a mother-of-pearl scaled tail. Russo was attracted. She sat down there and put their dirty bottle to her mouth and the black-rimmed fingernails of one of them fondled her neck. Russo heard their wheedling, brawling, booze-snagged voices calling and became a female along with the other unwashed three. We saw her scratching herself when she did still turn up— irregularly—to teach us Greek poetry. Did she share their body-lice too?

It was through her, perhaps, that real awareness of the people down there came. The revulsion and the pity; the old white woman with the suffering feet ganging up with the black ones when the men turned on the women in the paranoia of be-trayal—by some mother, some string of wives or lovers half-drowned in the bottles of the past—and cursing her sisters when one of them took a last cigarette butt or hung on a man the white sister favoured; tended by the sisterhood or tending one of them when the horrors shook or a blow was received. The stink of the compost heaps they used drifted through the libraries with the reminder that higher functions might belong to us but we had to perform the lower ones just like the wretches who made us stop our noses. Shit wasn't a meaningless expletive, it was part of the hazards of the human condition. They were ugly, down there at the grandstands and under the bushes, barnacled and scaled with disease and rejection, no-one knows how you may pick it up, how it is transmitted, turning blacks grey and firing whites' faces in a furnace of exposure, taking away shame so that you beg, but leaving painful pride so that you can still rebuff, *I don't eat rubbish*, relying on violence because peace has to have shelter, but sticking together with those who threaten you because that is the only bond that's left. The shudder at it, and the freedom of it— to let go of assignments, assessments, tests of knowledge, hopes of tenure, the joy and misery of responsibility for lovers and children, money, debts. No goals and no failures. It was enviable and frightening to see them down there—Bester, Franklin-Turner, Heimrath and the others, Russo pulling herself to rights to play the goddess when she caught sight of us but too bedraggled to bring it off. Jepson, our Jepson, all that we had to believe in of the Old Guard's world, passing and not recognising us.

And then one day, they had simply disappeared. Gone. The groundsmen had swept away the broken bottles and discarded rags. The compost was doused with chemicals and spread on the campus's floral display. The Vice-Chancellor had never joined the bent backs round the zol and the bottle down there and was in his panelled office. The lines caging Heimrath's mouth in silence did not release him to ask why students gazed at him. Minerva sat before us in her special way with matched pale narrow hands placed as if one were the reflection of the other, its fingertips raised against a mirror. Jepson's old bristly sow's ear sagged patiently towards the discourse of the seminar's show-off.

From under the bushes and behind the grandstands they had gone, or someone had found a way to get rid of them overnight. But they are always with us. Just somewhere else.

THE DIAMOND MINE

I'll call her Tilla, you may call her by another name. You might think you knew her. You might have been the one: him. It's not by some simple colloquial habit we 'call' someone instead of naming: call them up.

It was during the war, your war, the Forties, that has sunk as far away into the century as the grandfathers' Nineteen-Fourteen. He was blond, stocky in khaki, attractively short-sighted so that the eyes that were actually having difficulty with focus seemed to be concentrating attentively on her. The impression is emphasized by the lashes blond and curly as his hair. He is completely different from the men she knows in the life of films—the only men she knows apart from her father—and whom she expected to come along one day not too far off, Robert Taylor or even the foreigner, Charles Boyer. He is different because—at last—he is real; she is sixteen. He is no foreigner nor materialisation of projection from Hollywood. He's the son of friends of a maternal grandmother, detailed to a military training camp in the province where the girl and her parents live. Some people even take in strangers from the camp for the respite of weekend leave; with a young daughter in the house this family would not go so far as to risk that but when the man of the family is beyond call-up age an easy way to fulfil patriotic duty is to offer hospitality to a man vouched for by connections. He's almost to be thought of as an elective grandson of the old lady. In war these strangers, remember, are Our Boys.

When he comes on Friday nights and stays until Sunday his presence makes a nice change for the three, mother, father and young daughter who live a quiet life, not given to socialising. That presence is a pleasant element in the closeness between parents and daughter: he is old enough to be an adult along with them, and only eight years ahead of her, young enough to be her contemporary. The mother cooks a substantial lunch on the Sundays he's there; you can imagine what the food must be like in a military camp. The father at least suggests a game of golf—welcome to borrow clubs, but it turns out the soldier doesn't play. What's his game, then? He likes to fish. But this hospitality is four hundred miles from the sea; the soldier laughs along in a guest's concession of manly recognition that there must be a game. The daughter—for her, she could never tell anyone, his weekend presence is a pervasion that fills the house, displaces all its familiar odours of home, is fresh and pungent: he's here. It's the emanation of khaki washed with strong soap and fixed, as in perfume the essence of flowers is fixed by alcohol, by the pressure of a hot iron.

The parents are reluctant cinema-goers, so it is thoughtful of this visiting friend of the family that he invites the daughter of the house to choose a film she'd like to see on a Saturday night. She has no driving licence yet (seventeen the qualifying age in those days) and the father does not offer his car to the soldier. So the pair walk down the road from streetlight to streetlight, under the trees, all that autumn, to the small town's centre where only the cinema and the pub in the hotel are awake. She is aware of window dummies in the closed shops her mother's friends patronise, observing her as she walks past with a man. If she is invited to a party given by a schoolfriend, she must be home strictly by eleven, usually fetched by her father. But now she is with a responsible friend, a family connection, not among unknown youths on the loose; if the film is a nine o'clock showing the pair are not home before midnight, and the lights are already extinguished in the parents' bedroom. It is then that, schoolgirlish, knowing nothing else to offer, she makes cocoa in the kitchen and it is then that he tells her about fishing. The kitchen is locked up for the night, the windows are closed and it is amazing how strong that presence of a man can be, that stiff-clean clothing warmed—not a scent, not a breath, but, as he moves his arms graphically in description of playing a catch, coming from the inner crease of his bare elbows where the sun on manoeuvres hasn't got at the secret fold, coming from that centre of being, the pliant hollow that vibrates between collar-bones as he speaks, the breast-plate rosy down to where a few brownish-blond hairs disappear into the open neck of the khaki shirt—he will never turn dark, his skin retains the sun, glows. Him.

Tilla has never gone fishing. Her father doesn't fish. Four hundred miles from the sea the boys at school kick and throw balls around—they know about, talk about, football and cricket. The father knows about, talks about, golf. Fishing. It opens the sea before her, the salt wind gets in the narrowed eyes conveying to her whole nights passed alone on the rocks. He walks from headland to headland on dawn-wet sand, the tide is out—sometimes in mid-sentence there's a check, half-smile, half-breath, because he's thinking of something this child couldn't know, this is his incantation that shuts out the smart parade-ground march towards killing and blinds the sights the gun trains on sawdust-stuffed figures where he is being drilled to see the face of the enemy to whom he, himself, is the enemy, with guts (he pulls the intricately perfect innards out of the fish he's caught, the fisherman's simple skill) in place of sawdust. Sleeping parents are right; he will not touch her innocence of what this century claims, commands from him.

Walking home where she used to race her bicycle up and down under the same trees, the clothing on their arms, the khaki sleeve, the sweater her mother has handed her as a condition of permission to be out in the chill night air, brushes by proximity, not intention. The strap of her sandal slips and as she pauses to right it, hopping on one leg, he steadies her by the forearm and then they walk on hand in hand. He's taking care of her. The next weekend they kiss in one of the tree-dark intervals between streetlights. Boys have kissed her; it happened only to her mouth; the next Saturday her arms went around him, his around her, her face approached, was pressed, breathed in and breathed against the hollow of neck where the pendulum of heartbeat can be felt, the living place above the breast-plate from which the incense of his presence had come. She was there.

In the kitchen there was no talk. The cocoa rose to top of the pot, made ready. All the sources of the warmth that her palms had extended to, everywhere in the house, as a domestic animal senses the warmth of a fire to approach, were in this body against hers, in the current of arms, the contact of chest, belly muscles, the deep strange heat from between his thighs. But he took care of her. Gently loosened her while she was discovering that a man has breasts, too, even if made of muscle, and that to press her own against them was an urgent exchange, walking on the wet sands with the fisherman.

The next weekend-leave—but the next weekend-leave is cancelled. Instead there's a call from the public phone at the canteen bar. The mother happened to answer and there were expressions of bright and encouraging regret that the daughter tried to piece into what they were responding to. The family was at supper. The father's mouth bunched stoically—Marching orders. Embarkation.

The mother nodded round the table, confirming.

She—the one I call Tilla—stood up appalled at the strength to strike the receiver from her mother and the inability of a good girl to do so. Then her mother was saying, But of course we'll take a drive out on Sunday, say goodbye and Godspeed. Grandma'd never forgive me if she thought . . . now can you tell me how to get there, beyond Pretoria, I know . . . I didn't catch it, what mine? And after the turn-off at the main road? Oh don't bother, I suppose we can ask at a petrol station if we get lost, everyone must know where that camp is, is there something we can bring you, anything you'll need . . .

It seems there's to be an outing made of it. Out of her stun: that essence, ironed khaki and soap, has been swept from the house, from the kitchen, by something that's got nothing to do with a fisherman except that he is a man, and as her father has stated—Embarkation—men go to war. Her mother makes picnic preparations: do you think a chicken or pickled ox-tongue, hard-boiled eggs, don't know where one can sit to eat in a military camp, there must be somewhere for visitors. Her father selects from his stack of travel brochures a map of the local area to place on the shelf below the windscreen. Petrol is rationed but he has been frugal with coupons, there are enough to provide a full tank. Because of this, plans for the picnic are abandoned, no picnic, her mother thinks wouldn't it be a nice gesture to take the soldier out for a restaurant lunch in the nearest city? There won't be many such luxuries for the young man on his way to war in the North African desert.

They have never shown her the mine, the diamond mine, although since she was a small child they have taken their daughter to places of interest as part of her education. They must have talked about it—her father is a mining company official himself, but the exploitation is gold, not precious stones—or more likely it has been cited in a general knowledge text at school: some famous diamond was dug there.

The camp is on part of the vast mine property, commandeered by the Defence Force, over the veld there are tents to the horizon, roped and staked, dun as the scuffed and dried grass and the earth scoured by boots—boots tramping everywhere khaki everywhere, the wearers replicating one another, him; where shall they find him? He did give a tent number. The numbers don't seem to be consecutive. Her father is called to a halt by a replica with a gun, slow-spoken and polite. The car follows given directions retained each differently by the mother and father, the car turns, backs up, take it slowly for heaven's sake.

She is the one: —There. There he is.

Of course, when you find him you see there is no-one like him, no bewilderment. They are all laughing in the conventions of greeting but his eyes have their concentrated attention for her. It is his greeting of the intervals between streetlights, and of the kitchen. This weekend which ends weekends seems also to be the first of winter; it's suddenly cold, wind bellies and whips at that tent where he must have slept, remote, between weekends. It's the weather for hot food, shelter. At the restaurant he chooses curry and rice for this last meal. He sprinkles grated coconut and she catches his eye and he smiles for her as he adds dollops of chutney. The smile is that of a greedy boy caught out and is also as if it were a hand squeezed under the table. No wine—the father has to drive, and young men oughtn't to be encouraged to drink, enough of that in the army—but there is icecream with canned peaches, coffee served, and peppermints with the compliments of the management.

It was too warm in the restaurant. Outside, high-altitude winds carry the breath of what must be early snow on the mountains far-away, unseen, as this drive in return to the camp carries the breath of war, far-away, unseen, where all the replicas in khaki are going to be shipped. No heating in the family car of those days, the soldier has only his thin, well-pressed khaki and the daughter, of course, like all young girls has taken no precaution against a change in the weather, she is wearing the skimpy flounced cotton dress (secretly chosen although he, being older, and a disciple of the sea's mysteries, probably won't even notice) that she was wearing the first time they walked to the cinema. The mother, concealing—she believes—irritation at the fecklessness of the young, next thing she'll have bronchitis and miss school—fortunately keeps a rug handy and insists that the passengers in the back seat put it over their knees.

It was easy to chat in the preoccupations of food along with the budgerigar chitter of other patrons in the restaurant. In the car, headed back for that final place, the camp, the outing is over. The father feels an obligation: at least, he can tell something about the diamond mine, that's of interest, and soon they'll actually be passing again the site of operations though you can't see much from the road.

The rug is like the pelt of some dusty pet animal settled over them. The warmth of the meal inside them is bringing it to life; a life they share, one body. It's pleasant to put your hand beneath it; the hands, his right, her left, find one another.

you know what a diamond is, of course, although you look at it as something pretty a woman wears on her finger mmh? well actually it consists of pure carbon crystallized

He doesn't like to be interrupted, there's no need to make any response, even if you still hear him. The right hand and left hand become so tightly clasped that the pad of muscle at the base of each thumb is flattened against the bone and the interlaced fingers are jammed down between the joints. It isn't a clasp against imminent parting, it's got nothing to do with any future, it belongs in the urgent purity of this present.

the crystallization in regular octahedrons that's to say eight-sided and in allied forms and the cut and polished ones you see in jewellery more or less follow

The hands lay together, simply happened, on the skirt over her left thigh, because that is where she had slipped her hand beneath the woolly comfort of the rug. Now he slowly released, first fingers, then palms—at once awareness signals between them that the rug is their tender accomplice, it must not be seen to be stirred by something—he released himself from her and for one bereft moment she thought he had left her behind, his eight-year advantage prevailed against such fusion of palms as it had done, so gently (oh but why) when they were in the dark between trees, when they were in the kitchen.

colourless or they may be tinted occasionally yellow pink even black

The hand had not emerged from the rug. She followed as if her eyes were closed or she was in the dark, it went as if it were playing, looking for a place to tickle as children do to make one another wriggle and laugh, where her skirt ended at her knee, going under her knee without displacing the skirt and touching the tendons and the hollow there. She didn't want to laugh (what would her father make of such a response to his knowledgeable commentary) so she glided her hand to his and put it back with hers where it had been before.

one of the biggest diamonds in the world after the Koh-i-noor's hundred-and-nine carats but that was found in India

The hand, his hand, pressed fingers into her thigh through the cotton flounce as if testing to see what was real about her; and stopped, and then out of the hesitation went down and, under the rug, up under the gauze of skirt, moved over her flesh. She did not look at him and he did not look at her.

and there are industrial gems you can cut glass with make bits for certain drills the hardest substance known

At the taut lip of her pants he hesitated again, no hurry, all something she was learning, he was teaching, the anticipation in his fingertips, he stroked along one of the veins in there in the delicate membrane-like skin that is at the crevice between leg and body (like the skin that the sun on manoeuvres couldn't reach in the crook of his elbow) just before the hair begins. And then he went under the elastic edge and his hand was soft on soft hair, his fingers like eyes attentive to her.

look at this veld nothing suggests one of the greatest ever, anywhere, down there, down in what we call Blue Earth the diamondiferous core

She has no clear idea of where his hand is now, what she feels is that they are kissing, they are in each other's mouths although they cannot look to one another.

Are you asleep back there?—the mother is remarking her own boredom with the mine—he is eight years older, able to speak: Just listening. His finger explores deep down in the dark, the hidden entrance to some sort of cave with its slippery walls and smooth stalagmite; she's found, he's found her.

The car is passing the mine processing plant.

product of the death and decay of forests millennia ago just as coal is but down there the ultimate alchemy you might say

Those others, the parents, they have no way of knowing. It has happened, it is happening under the old wooly rug that was all they can provide for her. She is free; of them. Found; and they don't know where she is.

At the camp, the father shakes the soldier's hand longer than in the usual grip. The mother for a moment looks as if she might give him a peck on the cheek, Godspeed, but it is not her way to be familiar.

Aren't you going to say goodbye? She's not a child, good heavens, a mother shouldn't have to remind of manners.

He's standing outside one of the tents with his hands hanging open at his sides as the car is driven away and the attention is upon her until, with his furry narrowed sight, he'll cease to be able to make her out while she still can see him, see him until he is made one with all the others in khaki, replicated, crossing and crowding, in preparation to embark.

If he had been killed in that war they would have heard, through the grandmother's connections.

Is it still you; somewhere, old?

HOMAGE

Read my lips.

Because I don't speak. You're sitting there, and when the train lurches you seem to bend forward to hear. But I don't speak.

If I could find them I could ask for the other half of the money I was going to get when I'd done it, but they're gone. I don't know where to look. I don't think they're here, anymore, they're in some other country, they move all the time and that's how they find men like me. We leave home because of governments overthrown, a conscript on the wrong side; no work, no bread or oil in the shops, and when we cross a border we're put over another border, and another. What is your final destination? We don't know; we don't know where we can stay, where we won't be sent on somewhere else, from one tent camp to another in a country where you can't get papers.

I don't ever speak.

They find us there, in one of these places—they found me and they saved me, they can do anything, they got me in here with papers and a name they gave me; I buried my name, no-one will ever dig it out of me. They told me what they wanted done and they paid me half the money right away. I ate and I had clothes to wear and I had a room in a hotel where people read the menu outside three different restaurants before deciding where to have their meal. There was free shampoo in the bathroom and the key to a private safe where liquor was kept instead of money.

They had prepared everything for me. They had followed him for months and they knew when he went where, at what time—although he was such an important man, he would go out privately with his wife, without his State bodyguards, because he liked to pretend to be an ordinary person or he wanted to be an ordinary person. They knew he didn't understand that that was impossible for him; and that made it possible for them to pay me to do what they paid me to do.

I am nobody; no country counts me in its census, the name they gave me doesn't exist: nobody did what was done. He took time off, with his wife by the arm, to a restaurant with double doors to keep out the cold, the one they went to week after week, and afterwards, although I'd been told they always went home, they turned into a cinema. I waited. I had one beer in a bar, that's all, and I came back. People coming out of the cinema didn't show they recognised him because people in this country like to let their leaders be ordinary. He took his wife, like any ordinary citizen, to that corner where the entrance goes down to the subway trains and as he stood back to let her pass ahead of him I did it. I did it just as they paid me to, as they tested my marksmanship for, right in the back of the skull. As he fell and as I turned to run, I did it again, as they paid me to, to make sure.

She made the mistake of dropping on her knees to him before she looked up to see who had done it. All she could tell the police, the papers and the inquiry was that she saw the back of a man in dark clothing, a leather jacket, leaping up the flight of steps that leads from the side-street. This particular city is one of steep rises and dark alleys. She never saw my face. Years later now, (I read in the papers) she keeps telling people how she never saw the face, she never saw the face of the one who did it, if only she had looked up seconds sooner—they would have been able to find me, the nobody who did it would have become me. She thinks all the time about the back of my head in the dark cap (it was not dark, really, it was a light green-and-brown check, an expensive cap I'd bought with the money, afterwards I threw it in the canal with a stone in it). She thinks of my neck, the bit of my neck she could have seen between the cap and the collar of the leather jacket (I couldn't throw that in the canal, I had it dyed). She thinks of the shine of the leather jacket across my shoulders under the puddle of light from a street-lamp that stands at the top of the flight, and my legs moving so fast I disappear while she screams.

The police arrested a drug-pusher they picked up in the alley at the top of the steps. She couldn't say whether or not it was him because she had no face to remember. The same with others the police raked in from the streets and from those with criminal records and political grievances; no face. So I had nothing to fear. All the time I was being pushed out of one country into another I was afraid, afraid of having no papers, afraid of being questioned, afraid of being hungry, but now I had nothing to be afraid of. I still have nothing to fear. I don't speak.

I search the papers for whatever is written about what was done; the inquiry doesn't close, the police, the people, this whole country, keep on searching. I read all the theories; sometimes, like now, in the subway train, I make out on the back of someone's newspaper a new one. An Iranian plot, because of this country's hostility towards some government there. A South African attempt to revenge this country's sanctions against some racist government there, at the time. I could tell who did it, but not why. When they paid me the first half of the money—just like that, right away!—they didn't tell me and I didn't ask. Why should I ask; what government, on any side, anywhere, would take me in. They were the only people to offer me anything.

And then I got only half what they promised. And there isn't much left after five years, five years next month. I've done some sort of work, now and then, so no-one would be wondering where I got the money to pay the rent for my room and so on. Worked at the race course, and once or twice in night clubs. Places where they don't register you with any labour office. What was I thinking I was going to do with the money if I had got it all, as they promised? Get away, somewhere else? When I think of going to some other country, like they did, taking out at the frontier the papers and the name of nobody they gave me, showing my face—

I don't talk.

I don't take up with anybody. Not even a woman. Those places I worked, I would get offers to do things, move stolen goods, handle drugs: people seemed to smell out somehow I'd made myself available. But I am not! I am not here, in this city. This city has never seen my face, only the back of a man leaping up the steps that led to the alley near the subway station. It's said, I know, that you return to the scene of what you did. I never go near, I never walk past that subway station. I've never been back to those steps. When she screamed after me as I disappeared, I disappeared for ever.

I couldn't believe it when I read that they were not going to bury him in a cemetery. They put him in the bit of public garden in front of the church that's near the subway station. It's an ordinary-looking place with a few old trees dripping in the rain on gravel paths, right on a main street. There's an engraved stone and a low railing, that's all. And people come in their lunch-hour, people come while they're out shopping, people come up out of that subway, out of that cinema, and they tramp over the gravel to go and stand there, where he is. They put flowers down.

I've been there. I've seen. I don't keep away. It's a place like any other place, to me. Every time I go there, following the others over the crunch of feet on the path, I see even young people weeping, they put down their flowers and sometimes sheets of paper with what looks like lines of poems written there (I can't read this language well), and I see that the inquiry goes on, it will not end until they find the face, until the back of nobody turns about. And that will never happen. Now I do what the others do. It's the way to be safe, perfectly safe. Today I bought a cheap bunch of red roses held by an elastic band wound tight between their crushed leaves and wet thorns, and laid it there, before the engraved stone, behind the low railing, where my name is buried with him.

AN EMISSARY

'. . . how few Westerners grasp malaria's devastation. That said, its global toll remains staggering. In the last 20 years, it has killed nearly twice as many people as AIDS. . . . Malarial mosquitoes can even stow away on international flights— just ask recent unsuspecting victims near airports in Germany, Paris and São Paulo.'

All impurity hazing away, middleage evanescing, you can't really make out their jowls and eye-pouches in the steam, and your own face if you could see it would be smudged, all that you've done to it, the wriggles of red veins down the nose, wafted from view. Underneath is you as you were.

This place calls itself Fredo's Sauna and Health Club. But when you're lying here you're a senator among senators and nobles in a Roman bath. It's winter now—no need to worry, no dangerous ultra-violet striking you, nothing noxious survives. Winter now but there's no shivering here! Never any winter. In the humidity summer lives on; and there's some tiny thing floating out off the misty heat—can't be—no, must be a shred of someone's towel—but it lands on a plump wet pectoral, just above the hair-forest there, it's alive—and now dead, smack! A deformed punctuation mark of black, a scrap of wing, sliding on sweat.

Winter outside but there's water and privacy for breeding, eggs to lie low where no-one could imagine it, a place in which to emerge as you were, sloping back, transparent wings and special proboscis feature, in Fredo's Sauna and Health Club.

The musical conversation of the orchestra, tuning up rather like athletes running-on-the-spot and shadow-punching, before performance; it even includes the pitch of anticipation in the low interchange of human voices. A diminuendo from this audience, as the musicians come from the wings, and a rallentando when the guest conductor, a famous young Czech or whatever, appears to bow, turn his back, mount the podium and settle his shoulders in readiness to enter the symphony with raised baton.

It's winter, but nobody coughs. The sonority of wind, strings and keyboard calms all, the following tempest of brass sweeps away all reactions but the aural. The cello and viola file into the temple of each ear with the intoning of monks, there's the query of the flute, the double-stopping grunt of the bass, the berating of drums and an answering ping of a triangle. All these creatures produce the beauty of the invisible life of sound. They dive, they soar, they ripple and glide almost beyond the reach of reception, and swell to return; some overwhelm others and then in turn are subsumed, but all are there somewhere in the layers of empyrean they ravishingly invade and transmute. They weave in and out of it, steal through it, flow into eight hundred sets of ears—it's a full house when this conductor comes out on tour from one of those dangerous benighted Balkan countries that are always seceding and fighting and changing their names.

The auditorium is kept welcomingly heated by artificial means and by the pleasant warmth of human breath. A minute manifestation of being flies with the music, contributing a high, long-drawn fiddle-note. Nobody hears this Ariel materialise round their heads.

On the other hemisphere—Southern—it is summer, not simulation that makes all the year a summer.

They are not here officially, driving on a rutted muddy road between baobab trees, if officially means that your whereabouts are known to close collaterals—wives, husbands, and professional partners. An irresistible mutual impulse—like the original unlikely one that brought them together—to take to themselves something more than two hours once a week under an assumed name in an obscure hotel, had discovered in each the ability to devise unbelievably believable absences, the call of professional commitments. They took a plane, carefully not travelling even in the same class (how clever passion makes even those who have been honest and open all their lives). They chose an unlikely destination—they hoped; in their circles people travel a lot

WINGED
CHARIOT

145

and quite adventurously, so long as the camps are luxury ones with open-air bars and helicopter service.

The baobabs are mythical animals turned to stone.

Whenever before would he have found himself beside a woman who would come out with such delightful fantasies! She's a writer, and sees everywhere what he has never seen; he's an economist, privy to so much about the workings of the world she always has felt herself ignorant of, and here he is, listening with admiration to her trivial knack of imagery.

This adventure of theirs can only last a few days—the credibility of the alibis won't allow longer—and it has come late and totally unexpected, to both of them. Husband, wife, half-grown children, reputation—now a last chance: of what? Something missed, now to be urgently claimed. He loves her to speak poetry to him as he drives. It's her poetry, appropriated by her to accompany her life, the poets knowing always better than she does what is happening to her; now, to them. What they have done is crazy, the final destination a bad end; the realisation comes silently to each with a bump in the rutted road. Then she's saying for them both, as the medium possessed by a dead poet, the lines don't all reach her in the right sequence—at my back I always hear, Time's wingèd chariot hurrying near . . . let us roll all our strength and all our sweetness up . . . and tear our pleasures with rough strife through the iron gates of life . . . the grave's a fine and private place but none I think do there embrace . . .

He swerves to the side of the deserted road and turns off the ignition. They stare at each other and he breaks the spell with a smile and slow-moving head, side-to-side. There's no-one, nothing to witness the embrace, the struggle of each not to let go. Then he suddenly frees himself, gets out of the car, opens the passenger door and takes her by the hand. There are old puddles, soupy with stagnation, to step across. The sagging remains of a broken fence: whose land was this, once. No-one, nothing. The sun rests on their backs as a benign hand, they walk a little while over stubble, viscous hollows bleary with past rain, and cannot walk farther, are arrested by need. And there is some tree that really is a tree, in leaf over a low mound of tender grass grown in its moist shelter.

Lying there they find their way to each other through their clothes like any teenagers making love wherever they can hide. It doesn't matter. Now they lie, breathing each other in, diastole and systole, and nothing draws near, there is only that indefinable supersonic humming of organic and insect life, the sap rising in the tree, grass sprouting, gauze of gnats hovering, and a silent shrike swoops from a branch to catch some kind of flying prey in mid-air.

He is stirred, eventually, by past reality, in concern for her—remembering the hazards of hunting
trips he has taken: I hope there're no ticks. She
moves her head, eyes closed: no. Nothing. Safe.
Opens her eyes to see him, nothing else. One of the
flying specks has landed on the lobe of his ear, lingering there, while she blows at it. He starts with a
faint exclamation, she frees a hand and flicks whatever it is, so small, nothing, away.

SHOOTING
UP

The rave is in one of those four-walls-and-roof with
creaky boards that has housed all kinds of purposes—a church or school hall where there isn't, in
this neighbourhood, a church or school anymore,
and the toilets are across a yard that in the daytime
is used by some guys to repair exhausts. Dismem-
bered vehicle parts and gas cylinders have to be nav-
igated to reach where he's gone off to. There he is,
sitting on the broken seat, but he has his trousers on,
he's sure not having a shit, and his sweat-shirt sleeve
is rolled back on his bare white arm, he's got an arm
pale and hairless as a girl's. And just look at it.

I thought you'd kicked the habit.

He laughs. You want to use this seat?

But he allows the arm to be grasped.

Just see your arm.

What's one more prick? How can you tell one
from another, high yourself on booze.

So what's that on your arm?

Mosquito bite.
Very funny. Hahaha.

Summer, winter, Northern Hemisphere, Southern Hemisphere. There's nothing to be afraid of, nothing! A speck hovering, landing, you can swat with the palm of a hand. It's not the Reaper with the scythe.

It's his emissary, Anopheles.

KARMA

'Karma. . . . 1) The sum and the consequences of a person's actions during the successive phases of his existence, regarded as determining his destiny. 2) Fate, destiny. Sanskrit karman (nominative karma), act, deed, work, from karoti, he makes, he does.'

—THE AMERICAN HERITAGE DICTIONARY
OF THE ENGLISH LANGUAGE

'. . . so man is continually peopling his current space with a world of his own.'

Arthur's wife Norma is the one who is in the group photographs of conferences published in newspapers, she is
quoted on the radio and sometimes appears on a TV panel. They
have become a couple with a public profile, as the opinion polls
would show. He is in insurance, a steady position, wasn't doing
too badly even when they bought the place she set her heart on,
a bit beyond their means, then. It looked as if he might become
a general manager, eventually, some day—who knows, so they
could afford, in another sense, to begin to prepare a place equal
to status.

If you don't have ambitions when you're young what kind of
couple are you? She certainly had had ambition when she finished school top of her class. She'd wanted to go to university,
study political science, economics, subjects she'd heard about in
the company of her trade unionist parents and their friends, but
there was no money. She worked in a factory, in the offices of a
restaurant chain, picking up computer efficiency, studied her
chosen subjects by correspondence courses, and became one of
the working-class whites in the liberation movement. A resilient
thread in a net that operated Underground. The movement sent
her out of the country on a mission to one of their overseas offices while by some oversight on the part of the political police

she still had a passport; when she came back her name appeared on a list of banned persons: her movements and the kind of work she could do to earn a living were restricted.

It was when the leftish-liberal manager of an insurance company did the bravest thing he could steel himself to, and quietly took her on as a filing clerk, that she met Arthur. There are at least two magnetic sources of attraction in the process called falling in love. (Anyone can think of a number of others.) The face, body, of the object-individual: that can be enough. The personality: it may make the above irrelevant. Arthur had no specific sexually-aesthetic taste in what was beauty in a woman, girls were pretty or ugly or just somehow inbetween. Norma, short, with a business-like body (characterised always about some movement and task) and a face in the inbetween category, could not have started the process by means of the first magnetic source. Arthur fell in love, deeply appreciative, with the force of her personality. She was everything he had never been, done everything he had never done. He was one step up out of the working-class from which she came. His father owned a small printing business where his mother acted as receptionist-bookkeeper, they kept clear of politics; the discount price of their middle-class white security, dependent on the local government's orders for certain forms, might be withdrawn. Arthur was brought up to be honest about money, kind, to respect other people, no matter who or what they were, but without getting mixed with their ideas or problems; make his way as his parents had had to do—for himself. The insurance company was a good start. Whatever happened. In the country. There would always have to be insurance for people's possessions, against other people who took these from them.

That was life as proposed to him. Yet he read the newspapers, he came face to face with demonstrations prancing anger in the streets, their assault by police with dogs and guns, he saw, in his work at the insurance company, who owned everything in the country. So he refrained from using his privilege, as a white, to vote in the elections while others did not even have the right to demonstrate in the streets. That was his only political stance. He did not tell his parents they were wrong, he himself was wrong to accept skin privilege, do nothing about this but refuse a vote, making his way with the secret justification to himself that when the great change that was coming *did* come, he would welcome it and claim self-respect not to be found alone in making your way.

In love with Norma. She was evidence against himself and taking her for his own absolved him from however, whatever he had failed.

Arthur was good-looking, no inbetween so far as male beauty is concerned, and that may well have been the magnetism by which Norma was drawn, in love with him. Beauty has an innocence, it can't be aimed or plotted or struggled for as justice; it's a kind of assurance for someone who has lived with the deviousness, the machinations of survival, spied upon, hunted under bans.

Arthur was there for her, when it was all over—the bans, the head-hunters of the old regime disarmed of power. With his knowledge of the practical ways, the signals of a normal life of private ambitions and satisfactions she had not known, now legitimately open to those who had sacrificed for it, they could create a *new* normal life in the conditions of freedom. She had dossed down with comrades in places sleazy or disguised behind

a facade of respectability; he had lived past twenty with his parents and then, by the time he met her, in a bachelor flat whose
window was an inescapable observation post for the blare and
turmoil of a street of bars, minicabs hooting for custom, laughter and anger of pimps and prostitutes of three sexes. A job had
been found for her—the comrades kept one another in touch
about opportunities—with some non-governmental organisation taking care of the children and youths whose fathers had
died in action in the liberation forces or whose parents had disappeared in exile. He, of course, was secure in insurance, a necessity of the old normal life that, as his parents' wisdom had
predicted, remained a necessity in the new. Weekends and after
work almost every day they went looking at houses. A house of
your own; that always was and always will be the beginning of
the normal life they were set upon: she deserved. Estate agents
lied to them; they quickly became wise to the basic questions
with which to counter: was the highly-praised house on offer not
too near a freeway, was the nearby green space one where homeless people put up shacks, was there a creche in the suburb
(Norma was expecting their first child), what was the crime rate
in the area?

Finally, they found the house for themselves. They were driving around a neighbourhood they had heard about from black
friends of Norma who were moving, now, out of the black townships become ancestral homes to flee. Norma saw the Cape
Dutch gable. A house with character! He was privately surprised
at her enthusiasm for an architectural embellishment that was
the style, brought from Holland, by the forefathers of the people
who had spied upon, pursued and banned her from her rights,
imprisoned and tortured her kind. But it is true that a gable is

graceful; it makes a house unique among others in what was the kind of street they visualise starting out on. Jacaranda trees all along both sides. And there was a For Sale notice on the gate. They raised a bond on the evidence of his position advancing at the insurance company, and bought the Cape Dutch gable and all that was behind it, wonderful, more rooms than they'd need, but they were going to have a family, he'd earned his promotion from dreary bachelordom and she hers from anonymous hideouts.

Arthur lies in bed on weekend mornings at leisure and his mind wanders visually through the house and garden. He is not thinking, there are no words. There is the livingroom ceiling, generations of thick hard paint removed to reveal gold-brown lengths of wood panelling, hooded angle lights shining down from it softly. (Real style; the architect who was a colleague on the urban planning commission with Norma discovered for them the original fine pine under the paint.) The mounting pink profusion of Bauhinia he'd planted, rambled over by purple-blue Morning Glory at the boundary where the old trees were too dark a conclusion to the north end of the garden. The semicircle of blond cane with clean glasses on its table-top, striped in terrace sunlight—his hospitality bar. Green of the lawn well-kept by the black weekly gardener and green of the mini billiard table in what's come to be called the TV room since the two kids like to watch programmes adults can't sit through. That passing vision, with Norma and a glass of wine, after the day, watching the news on the other set in the livingroom. And transparencies of what isn't there yet. Still to come. One of those garden statues, cement but look like real stone, to glance at you from the centre of the lawn when you stand at the glass sliding doors he had installed in the livingroom soon as they could afford it, not long after they had moved in. One of the first to go through the doors: the baby just born, there in his pram. A swimming pool—where in the garden, imagined?—most people in the street have one but Norma won't agree because the child of friends drowned in theirs.

Norma bought him the mini billiard table as a surprise. Some connection through a firm that had tendered to the Commission for Sanitation in informal settlements (Norma had moved to Public Works, then) also owned a factory that made what they called entertainment equipment. It arrived on his birthday —But it must have cost a packet, Norma!—

—So what? Why shouldn't you have some fun, I've seen how you enjoyed yourself on the table at Edward's place. Anyway, I got a big discount.—

He taught their first-born, then seven years old, to play and as their arms grew longer it was used more and more by Danny and his schoolfriends. Danny was proud of it: if the school soccer game was washed out —Come to my house, we've got a real billiard table in our TV room.—

When they had lived almost nine years behind the Cape Dutch gable (you can't miss our place just look out for that when you come to the street) it was occupied in the patterns of their presence, their personal routes, invisible internal maps of existence from room to room, Norma and Arthur, Danny and his brother Brett. Almost completely occupied, but not quite. Still some to come: things to be achieved. The statue, a woman moulded with draping over one shoulder, was in place, and an electronic call system linked to the house was installed at the gates—Norma left Public Works to go into what was officially termed the Private Sector: individuals whose economic status put them at particular risk of thieving intruders and other invaders of privacy in their homes.

The Private Sector she joined was in fact the construction company one of whose directors she had come to know when the company tendered for a sanitation project in informal settlements. She became at once assistant to the director. Her salary and benefits were beyond anything she and Arthur could have imagined reaching, at first; but it is much easier to become accustomed to having money than it is to do without it. Norma had a natural aptitude that was perhaps already evident when first she saw the Cape Dutch gable and claimed its flourish for herself. There was a holiday in Europe, she saw some suppliers in an English industrial city and then she and Arthur took a Mediterranean cruise. Norma was orderly; kept every taxi receipt and credit card restaurant bill, don't bother about anything, it's routine entertainment allowance. The director's secretary at the company arranged air tickets for other, frequent travels where, if Arthur could absent himself from his insurance office, he was consort of the director's assistant. Through Norma's connections their elder son found a place at the most selective and expensive private school. The black maid who cleaned the house and did the family washing was placed under the supervision of a cook-housekeeper, also black; one of the directors had died and Norma, appointed to take his place, was too occupied with the demands of her position to have time or mind for shopping or cooking.

The couple's social life was extensive, expansive; not much use for Arthur's little home-built terrace bar. The company's public relations dinners and working breakfasts were eaten and libated in restaurants. Norma and her husband were guests at the national day celebrations of foreign embassies and the homes of Government officials, even a Minister in whose projects of urban renewal the company was involved, or expected to be. She bought Arthur silk shirts and a brocade cummerbund for important formal occasions; the couple came back through the electronic Open Sesame of their gates and made love in the house of their achievement. There was no question of jealousy; this need, hers of him, made Norma's success his as well, just as, when they met, she was everything he had never been, done everything he had never done. What he had done, was doing, was still in the process of creating, there's no end to it, is that containment of everything they are—Norma, himself, their children—which is home, the organism that expresses, and grows in, status.

Norma, of course, has changed outwardly with status. Reduced rather than grown . . . slimmed away the stockiness with diet, massage and the gym she insists they go to together; changed the colour of her hair and smoothed the bluntness of her face with beauty treatments, professional make-up before official occasions. She wears the female tycoon outfits of cross-dressing masculine suits with the jacket open over flouncy blouses which reveal the beginning of the valley between breasts. She has shed everything of the old days Underground, the dossing-down anywhere, the risky missions that mustn't be questioned, the hunter's eye of the Plain Clothes political police at the corner—everything but the bonding then, way back, with the comrades, many of whom are now in Government and parastatal organisations. That's still there: a new kind of Underground. To be counted on. The people who lost power have their sneering accusatory term for it: nepotism. As if they didn't do it, jobs for pals, in their day. But their pals had not suffered, had done nothing to deserve reward. Unless for their evil. And where in the world is there a political party in power, a government, that does not take the right to appoint its proven colleagues from the guerrilla times of opposition, parliamentary let alone revolutionary, to important cabinet portfolios and other high positions?

Norma was more than competent. There didn't need to be any snide justification cited for her appointment: she simply fulfilled every principle of the new order of fitness for public life and responsibility, even the professional scepticism of the newspaper editorials granted her highly intelligent use of experience gained in various sectors, and if she was not black, at least she qualified for that other, the gender principle industry as well as Government was expected to follow: she was a woman appointee. Often she was the Company board's choice to be negotiator on joint projects with the Government. That would be one of the occasions when her photograph would appear in the newspapers. When representatives of the World Bank or the Group of 8 visited the country official invitations came to her and her partner (secretaries had been instructed to avoid gender forms of address which stereotype the concept of a couple, there are dignitaries linked together as two men or two women). So sometimes Arthur was in the photograph, too, if half-hidden between other heads. At such gatherings there was always, naturally, the Minister or Minister's Deputy from Norma's old days who had put her on the list the important visitors should meet, be aware of. A consciousness that might be recalled some time, useful to the comrade become colleague, in her advancement.

The house with the Cape Dutch gable continued to keep up; the furniture that already had been changed since the basic stuff that was all they could afford when they moved in was replaced by something more comfortable and of better quality. Arthur caught his Norma looking about her, shifting in a chair, and it was as if he read it, said it for her. And for himself. —Shouldn't we look for one of those leather seating units you can move around, compose the way you like, you know, more places for people to group in.— Journalists came to interview Norma, TV crews were often there to film the encounter for overseas series seeking the opinions of prominent people outside Government but active in the progress of the country. There had also grown up the tradition, following that of other people living in their kind of suburb, of giving a quasi-official party on some private occasion—birthday or wedding anniversary. Norma would call in an Indian caterer, old comrade who had made his particular way to thrive in new circumstances.

—I love the feel of leather.— She seemed already to be arranging the units, this way or that, in their livingroom. They decided it was not worth the trouble to advertise furniture for sale and have people coming to view. The Cape Dutch gable was hardly the place for yard sales. They donated the old stuff to a shelter for the homeless aged Welfare told her about; a van came to take it away, there was a grateful letter from the trustees of the place, it was somehow nice to think that the acquisition of an indoor setting adequate to the distinction of the gabled facade of their life at this stage also benefitted others who had the misfortune to have descended to the nadir.

It was shortly after the new furniture had been put in place (how he and she enjoyed themselves trying out the combinations, a mating dance, with her pleasure at the smooth cling of the leather to her bare legs when he and she collapsed on the seats!) that the accident happened. She was driving from a late meeting. At the sharp turn off the main road that led to the quickest, familiar way to the Cape Dutch gable, a car came from somewhere—a blind blunder into her. Her car was flung away with the whole passenger side punched to a crumple. The impact was as if an invisible blow in the face but she was unhurt. And so was the driver of the other car. There followed the usual procedures, that Arthur took care of. Police report, wreck towed away, insurance claimed; his line. It was clear Norma was not at fault; but maybe neither was the other driver. The traffic lights were not functioning at the crossroads he came from; if anyone was culpable it was the city traffic department. One of the deficiencies of ordinary capacity in administration, now; the fascist-racists everywhere, anywhere, were always more efficient than the free.

She had a company car but it was being serviced that particular day and the car she was driving was their own, the family one—Arthur too, in his slow but satisfactory advance to Assistant General Manager had his company car. It's a man's affair, buying a car. A woman chooses the colour and has a preference for the profile, as the vehicles stand patient for acquisition in ballroom-showrooms, but the man looks under the hood and has a criterion of safety features and local availability of spares, to be met. Arthur visited dealers and brought home brochures. They studied them together, flipping with an admiring detachment past the ultimate luxury models but agreeing that they didn't want another station wagon, they had moved out of the utility class, the boys were old enough now not to climb on the seats and household supplies were delivered, not loaded and lugged from a supermarket. The decision was made for the latest good model in an upper price range (as the salesman placed it in his hierarchy) but not excessively high. So long as it had automatic transmission and the other requirements Arthur tried out on his test drive, the car was the right one to glide through the Open Sesame gates as one of the appropriate complements to what had been made, what was being made, of the home behind the gable. Norma wanted the colour to be blue; only black or red was on the dealer's floor, but a blue model would be available in a few days.

—Have you ordered it?— The question was her greeting as she flung down her briefcase and brushed his cheek as if he were a handkerchief passing her lips. —Because if you have, get on to the man and cancel. You haven't signed anything, no? We can get a wonderful deal.— She named one of the great foreign luxury cars whose photographs they had flipped through in brochures. A co-director knew the right dealer well and she would meet him next day. Yes, she was aware of the fortune a car like that cost, but she had been promised—absolutely—there'd be a sizeable discount. And almost nothing in cash on the spot. The colleague could assure anybody of her position in one of the two largest construction firms in the country, payments no problem. The dealers know it's good for their business to have prominent people choosing their make of luxury vehicle.

—Can you imagine yourself driving one of those!— As if he were a little boy with a dream to be fulfilled. Norma hugged him.

Later, after a happy, noisy meal with the boys—often their mother wasn't there, she had business engagements—and the children had gone to bed, she smiled her jaunty grimace-way from the old days. —Why shouldn't we take advantage of connections, like everybody else.—

The car was delivered. It was not blue but silvery and had the pedigreed scent of real leather seats, a console like that of the array of controls before the pilot of a plane. It was so long that it only just cleared the lowering of the roll-down doors in the garage. She was right, Arthur enjoyed driving the family on trips; when it was not in use, the pedigreed in its stable, it was another, an exalted attribute to the life being created in the house with the Cape Dutch gable Norma had chosen unerringly, that one look.

A year or more passed and Brett, the younger son, satisfactorily found a place along with his brother at the best of private schools. On the newspaper posters that couldn't be read as the Assistant Manager of an insurance company was urged along by rush hour traffic, but whose headlines filled the wait at red lights, news from the world was often ousted by terse assertions of local corruption. Corruption in central government departments, regional, provincial structures, privatisation projects, land redistribution, mining or fishing rights, airline mergers— land, sea and air—the very air that was being circulated by the vehicle's airconditioning. When he got home he read in the newspaper details of whatever the accusations and evidence were; and heard the assertions and denials on the radio, saw, with Norma over wine, the faces of those involved who consented to appear on TV to exonerate themselves in defence. Often the faces were those of official spokespersons rather than the individual him- or herself. It was so repetitive that it became if not boring—some of the names were fascinatingly unexpected—accepted, if within critical unease: a climate, a season. Living in it; not of it.

There was an evening unlike their evenings together with wine and television news. Norma switched off image and sound in mid-sentence. She sat with both hands round her glass looking into it.

Norma was not one for bad moods?

—Nothing. Problems at work.—

He mentioned a colleague of hers she had once spoken of as careless. She clicked her tongue in dismissal.

He waited, Norma always knew what she wanted to say and when. Timing was part of her efficiency, he admired how it had worked for her in her advancement.

—There's an investigation started into the finances of the Company. The Government tenders we won last year.—

—But it all went well. You were satisfied? The projects were completed according to specification and so on—I mean, the Company's not some little outfit taking on what it can't deliver.—

—It's the awarding of tenders. Who won the tender against others.—

Then it was flashed by on the newspaper posters in rush hour traffic, the latest scandal. CONSTRUCTION BECOMES CORRUPTION. He still believed it would be the members of the Board who would be investigated, and indicted if it were proved that bribery was involved in the awarding of contracts to the Company, though he was troubled about what this would mean for Norma's career. Muddy water splashes, anyone in insurance cases that come to Court knows that.

A weekly paper that relied on sensational exposé for its circulation published names and details of company corruption and Norma—Norma's name was among them. The pedigreed car she had bought at a 'discount', it is alleged (a newspaper has to be careful even if it has somehow found proof of a fact) was in recognition of the favour of putting in a good word to the ear of one of the members of the old comrades' bond in the Government department calling for tenders. The holidays Arthur had understood were complement to business trips or were paid for as her yearly bonus as a Director—these were her share of bribes between the Company and various tender boards' members with whom—wasn't that time honourably dead and buried—she had dossed down Underground.

The billiard table, the birthday present of the mini billiard table! That's where it started! If only he had realised then. And all the other achievements in his part of her advancement, the creation of the home for it behind the Cape Dutch gable—all carried out with the money in their joint bank account swelled by her. Directors in every kind of company award themselves bonuses when a company thrives, what was there to doubt in that? *Don't bother about anything it's routine business expenses.*

Arthur, for his part, through the insurance company knew good lawyers and engaged one to defend Norma in Court. The man insisted that he had obtained the best that could be expected: a heavy fine and suspended sentence, while two of the senior directors even lost their case on appeal to a higher Court and went to prison. Her background as a white who had suffered to bring about a just society, and the fact that she was female, the lawyer lectured, were the only mitigating factors in her favour.

—Your wife is a gullible woman. Or so the judge has chosen to believe.— And even if this had saved Norma, Arthur felt angry at the insult to her intelligence, all she had been and was. And there was bewilderment in him, at his anger: would he rather accept that his Norma was deviously dishonest?

It all happens just at the time when the architect has presented plans for extensions to the house that will not impinge upon or spoil the profile of the Cape Dutch gable against the sky. The boys have had lessons and are fine swimmers by now, there is a plan for a free-form pool and patio with change-room and bar with refrigerator.

They sold the house with the Cape Dutch gable, these things not accomplished, the home being made of it not fully achieved. The estate agent told them the property market was in decline; the Cape Dutch gable went at too low a price. It changed ownership several times in a decade.

'Aorist: Denotes past action without indicating completion, continuation.' Arthur: some years not long after, must have died; as the moment of that part of the process is termed.

'Many times man lives and dies,
Between his two eternities
That of race and that of soul.'

We were very excited when they told us about the new house. We knew there was something going on, the parents don't like to tell until something's sure because kids ask so many questions. But since my father's had his new big job, an office and every-

thing in what's called Regional Administration—whatever that
is—he talks with his friends, when they drink beer at our old
place, about rebuilding and clearing away street people and so
on—our mother's been greeting him with other long talk we
catch a few words of as we run in and out from playing in the
street.

Then they told us, my sisters and me, we are leaving Naledi
township, our grandmother's house where we were born, and
our grandmother's coming with us to live in a suburb. That's a
place where whites live. Now anyone can live there. It's not the
same suburb where the Catholic school is our father drove us to
on his way to his office in the city every morning; the school also
used to be for whites, but now any child can go there, my
mother says, long as the parents can pay high fees. The township
school is a dirty place and the teachers are lazy, she says. You can't
learn English properly there, and there's no hope of a good position like our father's, when you grow up, if you can't speak
proper English, it's the language of the world, she says.

So our uncle who has a transport business came with his re-
movals van and my friend Meshak, Rebecca, Thandike and I
helped the grownups load all our stuff. We also left some things
behind, that kind of rubbish isn't going to be what we need anymore, my mother said. Gogo still wanted her paraffin heater and
her funny old sewing machine. The sewing machine, all right.
My father lifted it in.

This house has rooms for everybody. Rebecca and Thandike
share because they want to, they say it's lonely to be by yourself.
But I like the room, my room, with all my things around, just
mine. I used to share with the girls in the township because
Gogo had to have a place. Our big TV that was squashed up

against the fridge in the room that was half-kitchen half-everything, the table and chairs and couch where we sat and ate our food and watched, looks the way it should be, here, in the room that has glass doors you can slide open. We kids sit on the carpet my father bought, thick and so wide and long it covers the whole floor, and that's how you can follow sport with my father in his new chair with its special rest for his feet up.

Our houses in the township were all the same except that some had a pretty door because people wanted them to look nicer. But in this street in the suburb all the houses are different. Mama says some are very old, they're built of stone, with an upstairs. Ours doesn't look as old as that and there's no upstairs, but in front you can't see the roof because of a kind of white wall—curly shapes, something like the head of our mother's and father's new bed—that sticks up into the sky from where you know the roof really begins. Rebecca says she's seen on TV houses like that when they show Cape Town and when she's said that, it reminds me—so that's where I must have seen what makes the house ours, that same wall. The feeling I get, where we've come to live now. There's no swimming pool yet, my father says maybe next year. There's a garden, all the houses in this street have these gardens, there's a kind of lady made of stone or something standing where you can see right down the grass to the flower bushes and high trees from the glass doors that slide away. Plenty of room to play. But we don't play there much. Mama tells us to but we don't. We always used to play in the street in Naledi. There wasn't a garden. In the garden you don't see anybody. When we come home from school we sit around under the street trees on the pavement with our feet in the road, same as always although in Naledi it was just the dust, no trees,

no smooth tar and gutters for the rain. Not many cars pass, just
the Watchem Security one that patrols looking for loafers and
thieves—Mama says everyone living on this street pays for this,
to be safe, our father too. The people in the other houses come
from work in super cars like my father's only even better, and the
gates of their places open by themselves, magic—we have gates
like that, as well, my father has in his car the whachamacallit he
presses to work them. There are other kids in the houses, white
kids. They play in the gardens of course. We don't know those
kids, they don't come out and tell us where they go to school,
what they're doing in those gardens. There's just one boy, lives
down the street, who comes out, riding his skateboard. He's not
black like us, he's an Indian boy you can see, black the sort of
way they are, so although his family have moved from the Indians' townships to the suburb, like us, he also doesn't know the
white kids. He's begun to come and sit where we fool around
and watch him fly past, him showing off a bit. He never offers to
lend me his skateboard. Thandike would be scared but Rebecca's
cheeky, she's asked him and he said no, his parents don't allow
anyone to ride it but him. Because it's dangerous, he says. And
he's only allowed to ride it on our street because it's a quiet one
and the downhill is just enough, not too much. So he doesn't try
it out anywhere else—I've told him there are much faster runs in
the other streets, up and down hills in this suburb. I know. Because the very first day we came here, with Uncle Ndlovu's van
with our stuff, I was the first one to unload something, I climbed
in and dragged out my bicycle that I'd got from my father for
winning a merit prize at school at the same time he won his new
great job. I rode off straight away, Mama and Gogo yelling after
me, where're you going, you'll get lost, you don't know this

place. But I did know all these streets, which went where, and which one became that one, where to turn to reach this way back to recognise our new house with the fancy white front, or instead take another way. Like my bike had a map. Maps on the school walls. But they're foreign countries.

So I dare Fazeel—we've told our names, Rebecca and Thandike too—to skate along with me all over, sometimes the downhill I know makes him fly so fast he even overtakes me on my bike, it's a superbike, I can do all sorts of tricks on it, now. He jumps and lands smack on his board that's running away from him, I pedal full-power, hands off, we zigzag round each other, the girls shout and laugh at us. It's real fun. And all the time it's in English, Fazeel wouldn't understand us in Sesotho, we're talking English every day at school and anyway where we live it's the language of everyone, the one for the suburb, we hear the voices of the white people we don't know, in their gardens. My dad (that's what we've got used to calling him in English instead of Tata, although our grandmother's still Gogo for us) also bought me a Superman helmet to wear when I'm on my bike, it's yellow with red arrows. Rebecca loves it and I let her wear it sometimes while she and Thandike run and dodge around Fazeel and me when we're having a competition in the fastest streets. I ride such a lot I'm getting to be a star, I could go on TV with the stunts I do. On the street where you can whizz down to the sharp corner that comes off from the main road, although you can't see it the five o'clock traffic's like the volume turned up full blast on a TV.

Look!

Fazeel's just done *something*!

Man! Man! But fabulous! He's jumped, turned himself right round, and landed back on the board! It's wobbling but he doesn't fall. The girls are shouting, Rebecca's dancing her bottom around, my helmet's too big for her, it's falling over her eyes, stupid, she must give it back but I must show Fazeel, I must show them all, everybody in our suburb where we're living, the streets I know—Look! Look! Look what I'm going to do now! They're yelling, So what! What you think you are! Laughing gasping because I'm no hands, I'm full speed, and I'm bending back, I'm looking up at them, show-off Fazeel, show-off silly girls, upsidedown. Now the bike's thrown me it's on top of my legs I'm on my elbow. I'm shouting *I'm okay, okay, don't touch me.* I'm going to get up right away. I'm going to get up but now there's a terrible noise the volume is up, on me, the underneath of a truck—

Sometimes the Return is such a short one.

Hardly worth it? No-one can know. No-one is ever to have such knowing. And if a Return is supposed to atone for errors, wrongs committed, acts uncompleted in a previous existence, how could I atone, sent back briefly as a life of a child to the streets, to the house with the fake Cape Dutch gable where something was not realised: awry, abandoned halfway.

'. . . sooner or later every action brings its retribution, in this existence or in one to come.'

C an you believe such a thing. Dump a baby in a toilet. Well it was the church toilet, whoever did it that Sunday knew when we brethren came to morning service we'd hear the crying. No-one could get hold of Welfare on a Sunday and the police— we know our police boys, they're our own sons or other relatives in our township, what'd they know about looking after a baby couldn't have been more than two weeks old! So Abraham and I took it home, just for the day, we don't have kids of our own and other brethren have the house full with them.

A girl. Pretty little thing. Had no hair yet just a bit of fine fluff, so what's the easiest thing you can tell whether a baby is one of us, tight, curly, wasn't there. Except for hair, most of our babies could be whites when they're born, they're very light-coloured, the white in us only gets taken over by the black as they get older. The noses usually aren't flatter than all babies have, and if the eyes are green—our grandfathers, great-grandfathers all the way back were Malay, Indian, Bushmen, real blacks, whites, you name it, and somehow from the mixture many of us have green eyes, like whites. By the time the Welfare made up their minds about which orphanage to get her into we'd . . . well, no kids of our own, we'd got fond of her, our life was different not just the two of us like before, Abraham had a good steady job with his Jewish boss at the shoe factory, I didn't really need to go out to work. So we kept her. We named her a lovely name, Denise, and gave her our name. She was christened in our Seventh Day Adventist church by our minister. It was only about the time she began to be steady on her feet and begin to walk that there was no doubt about it; she was a white kid. The reason why her hair was so fine and slow to cover was that she was going to be very blond. The green eyes didn't help; this kid was white. You do get throwbacks among us that can pass for white, but she was the real thing. Everybody saw it, all the neighbours and Abraham's and my aunties, uncles, cousins—and looked from the kid to us, saying nothing but thinking, we knew, what were we going to do, later? For school. The children played with her as if she was the same as them; children learn the names for difference, from us, what did apartheid mean to them: just another grown-ups' word. The local nursery school, run by our church with charity grants, was no problem. All shades of our skins passed, there, some were blacker than it was meant for, slipped in by parents from the nearby black township through family or church connections with our people; if one tot was whiter than she should be, who was going to ask questions.

But when the time came for *real* school, Government school, we had to make up our minds, Abraham and I. To be white in apartheid days was to be—everything. Everything! From, you know, sitting on a bench waiting for a bus, to getting a job in a bank, renting a flat, owning a house, qualifying in a trade, getting a good education—all these came to you, just like that, if you were white, all these were closed to you if you were some other colour. We had to decide whether our little girl—because who else's was she, she called us Mama and Daddy—should grow up to be one of us, our own people, here in the places and jobs, the lives the whites decide for us, or whether we owed it to her to try for white. And that's not the right way to put it, either, because that means you're not white but may be able to pass, and our girl *was* white. Easy to be accepted by our kind because what are we? Such a stew-pot most of us don't even know, from way back, what's made us whatever we are, our family names are only clues, Dutch, English, German, Jewish, Malay-Muslim, some of this is even hidden behind family names taken which are just names of months—September, February, that's two families in this street where Abraham and I took in what is called a foundling who had no name at all.

We decided to try to put her in a white school. That meant Government school was out. Government schools were separated: blacks at black schools, us coloureds at coloured schools, whites at white schools. Our child, living in our place, would have to go to the local school for our kind. But there were private schools we heard about. A convent school. We were Seventh Day Adventists, no whites or blacks in our local church, but people said the nuns had some arrangement, they took in a few black or coloured children if the parents could pay. But the convent refused her, the vacancies for exceptions were full, and then when we tried a private Anglican school, although the head-mistress who interviewed us with our child looked at her curiously and kind of sadly, she wasn't given a place there, either. The headmistress said that, even with us paying, the school couldn't afford to take our child because for coloured or black children the Government supplied no subsidy as it did for other private pupils.

Denise Appolis attended primary and high schools in a coloured township outside the city and suburbs, like the townships and schools designated for blacks and for Indians, and matriculated as head prefect with three distinctions, in English, Afrikaans (the language spoken in her home) and history. Abraham and Elsie Appolis were unsurprised and proud of her. There had grown up in them, as she grew up, the unspoken shared sense that because she was not their biological creation, she had not been made in their bed, she was somehow chosen. Not alone in the sense that they had taken her for a day and kept her; chosen for a different life, other than theirs. A life of fulfilment they thought of as happiness. Had they, then, not been happy? Yes, in their way, the way open to them. Happiness as being white: no boundaries! God's will.

Now it was possible for her to be what she was: white. The private business schools in the city were given as her home address that of Abraham's white Jewish boss (appropriated, with or without consent?) when Abraham and Elsie sent her for application unaccompanied by their presence and obvious place in the official race classification. She carried a letter of parental authority written carefully in English (corrected by the girl who had gained Distinction in that subject), and proof of the parents' ability to pay fees, in details of their savings bank account. There she was, a white seventeen-year-old among other young white men and women. She evidently made no friends but concentrated on her computer and general secretarial courses and every day came home by way of one of the roving minibuses in the city, back to the township, her friends there. Just as well she was the quiet one who kept to herself at the business college, she didn't bring any fellow student home; Abraham and Elsie never brought up the subject, neither did she offer any explanation.

It seemed she understood what their love was doing for her. You couldn't grow up in that township without becoming aware that it was best to be white, if by some good fortune you had the chance to take. God's will. When her courses were—successfully—completed she and the parents studied together the situations vacant advertised in the morning and evening papers; for the first time in his life Abraham brought home both (TV was the source of news for what was happening in the world, for him) from his boss's office, with the permission and kindly interest of his Jewish employer. After all, they were family men of around the same age; there was the joking: —You're not going down those pages because you're walking out on me?— —No, no . . . it's my daughter, just come through business college.—

Denise wrote her own confident letters of application, now giving the post office box number of her father's workplace for convenient reply. She read the format out to the parents for approval, and was granted several interviews in favourable response. With her very first job she could choose! Their Denise! Again the three conferred, Denise and the parents; Abraham knew something of the business world, even if he was only a factory foreman. She made the right choice: a trainee in a bank. All personnel white like her. Her starting salary was low, but enough for their girl to clothe herself, pay for daily minibus transport, enjoy a little independence, and it meant Elsie didn't have to take care of an old white lady anymore—work she'd found to help pay the business school fees. But it appeared that their girl had made one friend during the business school courses, after all. Denise's appointment at the bank was to begin on the first day of the coming month, two weeks ahead; she was having a holiday, a reward she deserved after her success in her courses, helping Elsie at home to make new curtains and riding into the city quite often to see the friend. She even spent a night at the friend's family house, there was a party. In the white suburbs, they were, house and party, of course.

Abraham found the words after he and Elsie were in the dark in bed. —D'you think she's told this friend.— —Told what.— As if there was nothing that would come out, nothing to explain. —Who she is. Us. Here.— —Must have. Otherwise what'd the friend think of never being invited back. Here.—

There was no resentment or hurt in the fact that their girl did not bring her friend home to them. Other play-whites did so, they knew, with genuinely trusted white pals, in particular that band of whites, Communists, Lefties, Liberals of one kind or another who wanted to prove themselves against the race laws. But their girl was not a play-white. She was fully entitled to be at those parties in the suburbs, sleeping over in a white's house. They knew and their girl knew what they wanted for her and she should claim for herself in order to fulfil that want.

Yet when she told them, she and her girlfriend had found a bachelor flat in the city they could afford and would be moving in together—it was the home address she'd given to the bank— they felt something suddenly fallen away from them. Under the very ground they themselves had prepared. That feeling, in their hanging hands, on their faces: it was so—so what? Unreasonable. Shaming. Silly. What on earth was the matter with them, you Abraham (her look), you mama Elsie (his look)? This was the next, the right and vital step in moving out of the cramped life they had and into the life that had everything. For her to leave them was the natural process of their act of love for her. Freed.

The friend Angela had found a job in an attorney's office near the bank, the housing arrangement was convenient for both and they got along well together. Abraham and Elsie drew some of their small savings to help Denise buy a refrigerator and her share of the basic furniture needed. They were taken to see the flat and met the girl Angela; it was clear she knew what to expect and was friendly and respectful in the normal way of young adults meeting someone's parents. So this girl Angela was in the compact as well. They never visited the flat again; but Denise came home—must still be home, a flat that's passed from occupant to occupant, marks on the walls not your own, can't be home—she came to them often. Nearly every Sunday, Christmas and birthdays, theirs and hers (calculated as the Sunday she was found in the church toilet), sometimes sleeping the night in her old bed. Such a good girl. Others with her circumstances would have disappeared, disowned them. And that they would have understood as the final act, in their love. God's will. If he allowed the laws—laws that made it necessary—to be the acts of people who prayed obedient to him in their whites' churches. This was a proviso that Abraham, growing older, had but would not pass on to Elsie, wounding her with his lapse of faith. Oddly, if there was anyone he might have conveyed it to it could have been his Jewish boss, he'd been working at the factory for more than twenty-five years and it was to himself, the foreman, that the boss one day confided he hadn't been away ill for a week, his absence was because he had been taking his wife back and forth to doctors for tests that showed she had cancer.

A foundling. Who was this girl they decided was Denise? A chosen one, having no provenance, she could make for herself two lives, one where she was cradled and loved and learnt to talk, communicate in the intimate *taal* of a designated township, learnt to walk—walk out into the second, other life: everything.

Denise and her flatmate had boyfriends. Angela, many. The weekends when Abraham-and-Elsie's girl was home with them, the current chap could come and make love to Angela in the flat. She never let on—that was the phrase her best friend could be assured of—where that conveniently absent best friend was. Denise, after a few trials that didn't get as far as bed, had only one boyfriend. When she knew Angela would be out for a late night, they could go to bed in the room she shared with Angela; their turn to make love. They had met at a party, the customary first stage in the white middle-class ritual of mating choices— the birthday of one of the other girls who worked in the bank. He was a technician with a company selling and servicing televi- sion sets; a young man from the lower end of that class, his fa- ther a retired post-master. Afrikaans was the home language but the mother was of English-speaking origin, so he was fluent in both, and attractively intelligent. A bee scenting something in her pollen: he lent books to his girl; they were there beside her bed when he wasn't and Angela was sleeping off wine and a wild night. They were novels and travel books. He was saving for a trip overseas, he knew what he wanted to see in his life, London, Paris, Rome. And Venice, she would add; one of the books de- scribed the Piazza San Marco, and the gondolas. Who, of either of them, could have said what decided they would marry—the love-making in her bed, the freedom beyond that she had gained for herself, the freedom he was aware of, the world outside the country, the city of a bank and a television sales shop? These were the components of falling in love; marriage was the accepted social means of protecting this and giving it permanence with an official license and vows in a church.

There the usual, simple progression of the mating ritual was neither usual nor simple. Denise had told Mike—not who she was because she didn't, couldn't know—who her Mama and Daddy were, and taken him back over the line she had crossed under their loving guidance, to meet them. He spoke Afrikaans with Abraham and Elsie, a common language brings ease, it didn't matter that the young white man was in a Coloured township, a Coloured home for the first time (a kind of foreign travel). Being in love is a state of the continuous present, the now; he was living only in the context of his girl's eyes and breasts and sweet thrilling entry to her body. This unfamiliar, forbidden separate place of colour she had been nurtured in was of no account to him; all that he had been nurtured to believe about the taint of contact with those of a different tint was irrelevant: being in love converted him from milk-imbibed racism, weaned him at a single encounter. And, of course, the fact was that his girl was not *theirs*, Abraham's and Elsie's, she was white—he knew better than anyone how white in all the physical characteristics cited by those claiming these as superior to the characteristics of all others in the official racial categories laid down by law and followed by the church. To record that Abraham and Elsie were overjoyed at a coming marriage of the girl who had been their Denise to a good young white man with a steady job (his own family speaking Afrikaans—a kind of link even though there probably wouldn't be the usual parents-in-law one) would be to understate the solemnity of that joy. First they had let her go; now the foundling had been found by one of her own kind. Everything: it was about to be achieved with this marriage.

He had to explain to his girl that her introduction to his parents might not be without certain problems. She looked at him as if he'd had a sudden lapse of memory. She'd been taken to their home several times, first fruit juice and beer on the verandah, where the mother talked to her about what it was like to work in a bank and the father talked to his son about soccer, then to lunch on a public holiday, and once to share the evening meal. —But that was before they knew—about you, I mean. I'd never thought it necessary to tell them about my girlfriends' families and so on. What interest to them. Nothing to do with their lives. Now when I say we're getting married, I'm marrying this girl, I'll have to tell them about you.—

—Of course.— But she had not thought of this before: love is in the present, it's her hand slipping beneath his shirt to his chest, it's reading together descriptions of the places in the world maybe they'll save up to see. She did not say: they know I'm white. As if he heard the thought: —I know . . . But that you grew up there, school and home, people who are like—your parents, to you.— He came over in her silence and kissed her; he had no part in the problem his parents might represent.

He came back with the news, angry, the skin over his cheekbones taut and flushed. —They're terrible. I don't even want to tell you about it. I'm degrading never mind myself, *them*, my sister, her kids. The country. Beautiful South Africa 1975. It doesn't matter to them that you're white. You were brought up among Coloureds, the family—which I've explained over and over again you haven't really got although you love them—is Coloured. You'd think colour is something you can catch just by being among people. Infection, it's a disease.— His car was piled with a thrown-in muddle of clothes, shoes, books, soccer helmet, music cassettes. He left home and moved in with a friend. In servants' quarters converted to a cottage rented in someone's garden he had a room to himself where she could comfort him with love-making; she knew something of what it was like to leave behind you those who had been your parents.

They had each other, in love. They would get married. Sooner, now, an act of confirmation, even of defiance, as well as love. But if he was angry before, he was stricken, transformed by disbelief when he came back from the marriage licence office to tell her that the licence was not, could not be issued. There would have to be a birth certificate to prove she was white; he could give his date and place of birth, the names of his parents. She had no birth certificate and no place except a church toilet, and her adoptive parents had registered her in their name and residence as Coloureds in a duly designated township. Denise Appolis was a Coloured female. The Mixed Marriages Act forbade marriage between them. Even their love-making was clandestine contravention of the law.

The television technician had never needed a lawyer, he was an ordinary law-abiding young man who wanted to marry in the usual progression of life, and, white and sure of his own, he had never taken any part in organisations concerned with human rights but remembered reading in newspapers of a legal aid resource that offered help in such matters. There he was received by a rumpled, well-rounded woman lawyer who ran her hands up through her hair as if they were going over a story she'd heard in various versions many times. —I know, I know it's an awful prospect, but your 'intended' will have to go before the Population Registrar. We'll make an application for her to be reclassified. White. Don't think I'm doubting you in any way, but I must meet her, first.—

—You'll see for yourself. Whoever they are can't have any doubts.—

—The parentage questions—habitation, childhood—complicates things, even if the physical appearance seems to fit by their invented genetic standards . . . —

When there is trouble you take your shock home to those to whom you went with the hurt of grazed knees.

She took him with her to Mama and Daddy, Abraham and Elsie, there she was able to give way to tears and they wept with her, hugged the young white man who hadn't given her up but become confined, as they had been all their lives, in one of those cages of the law that made people species of exotic animals: he must understand—yes—he's in the whites' cage. And she, their girl? If the lawyer knows the procedure, everyone in the township knows how you must present yourself before it. Everywhere, close, there are families to whom nature—God's will—has produced one of a brood who could play for white, Abraham and Elsie could call in all manner of advice from friends, relatives, expert in *their* ways; lore unknown to any lawyer. Without papers, registered Coloured, the girl must present herself, to that bastard looking her over, as if the girl really *is* a play-white who must disguise herself. He'll only be convinced, by his model of a real white girl, if she gets herself up in the right way that they know, from experience, will succeed. She looks too—what's it—lady-like. He'll find it fishy. He's not used to that. He's used to letting pass—all right, got to make a few who do, just to show the law is good—the special kind of looks, it's like they're on a rubber stamp ready to his hand, he recognises as properly faked. How she must dress and make up—that's important. *Really* white, you must look; she and her boyfriend go swimming a lot, she's rosily-dark sunburned.

Who knew better than the aunties, cousins, neighbours how to deal with the law's servants, those white 'civil servants' that decided your life for you. On the day she and her future husband met the lawyer at the office of the Population Registrar she was heavily plastered with chalky makeup, as if she truly had mixed blood to conceal, her hair, which lately she had followed the craze of the girls at the bank to have cooked into a rippling Afro, was tortured even straighter, her blondness bleached even blonder, than these were naturally.

The lawyer from Legal Aid was appalled. She left the future husband standing in a corridor and rushed the girl to the women's toilet where, totally concentrated, exasperatedly wordless, she scrubbed the face with paper tissues from her briefcase and drew palms-full of liquid soap from a dispenser to finish the job. The clean shining face of a tanned white girl, pink around the nostrils, emerged and it was in this naked aspect that the foundling applicant entered the official's office accompanied by the woman lawyer. The future husband left behind the door: he could make out the voice but not the words of the lawyer explicating her client's claim. His lips moved on the words he would have used. And he would also have said what surely couldn't be denied by any Registrar, I love her, isn't there a right to love.

His girl and the lawyer were on the other side of the door a long time. He did not allow himself to look at his watch as if the hour might be an omen; good or bad. He could scarcely catch his girl's low voice and an indifferent-sounding growl of the official's questions was infrequent, impossible to follow.

They came out and the door closed on a moment when he saw the official with his chin pressed into a swag of flesh as he bent over papers on a desk. She was looking straight in front of her, not at him. The woman lawyer was slowly wagging her head, lips tight. Absence of documentation, the applicant's answers to where her parents lived, who they were, what school she was admitted to, recognised as a Coloured among Coloureds all her childhood—these criteria have decided that her classification cannot be changed to white. Application refused. Sorry. That was what the half-audible growl had been decreeing.

They wandered out into the forest of city in which they were abandoned strangers. The lawyer was guiding them, at their backs. —Let's go to my office and have some coffee.— What could she have to say to them there? Application for reclassification refused.

They don't know, but she receives in never-silenced memory her echo of what they are feeling; as a child, a life ago, in a German town called Dortmund she was turned away from school with a yellow star stuck to her dress. —Look, I have experience with these people.— A note taken of the afterthought: 'Sorry'. —I'm going to see him tomorrow.—

Mr van Rensburg was amiable: you again. Rose from his

chair, both sat down. Across the desk from one another, a level of understanding confidentially, professionally assumed. You know, I know. The girl is white. Years ago some other white girl dumped an unwanted infant on church premises. —A church for Coloureds, *ja.*— —Yes. But in those days, you'll remember, there was a poor whites' area only a few yards away across the veld. If it'd been a whites' church, the mother might have been discovered.—

And now he released himself to the assumed level of understanding. —Look. *Ag,* she's white, can't I see it for myself. Of course. Anyone can see it. A nice young man wants to marry her. Jesus, I see what she is. But it's the law it's my job. She can perhaps apply again. If you can dig up something from the orphanage or church or whatever she was found. Sorry.—

They're saving up now. Not to see the Tower of London, the Champs Élysées, Piazza San Marco in Venice, but to go away, for good. That's how they describe leaving a home they can't have.

Perhaps they've come back since all the laws that decided who she was, who he was, have gone, as the politicians and newspapers like to put it, into the dustbin, the rotten eggshells and beer cans, of history. Years ago now, by the time that is measured when you're in bodily manifestation. The names of those heroes who made the laws have even been taken off street signs and airports.

I must have been released from her—she must have died, somehow, young: you don't always keep, know, the moment when you were recalled; how it ended. But of all my Returns that one was unique, there never was anything like it! Because, each time, you are one manifestation, sent back to live out one life. But *that* Return was *in itself* two, I had come back twice over in the same enclosure within space that is a planet.

Denise—my pretty name they gave me because I didn't have one. I'm thinking in the *taal*; I was so happy among the other kids in the township, our own place, my Mama and Daddy giving me my Barbie doll and all her outfits, even a pearl necklace that broke and Mama threaded again, the prizes I got, top girl in class, the Sundays when the aunties and uncles and cousins came, we kids ran races, turned cartwheels, and stuffed ourselves with sweets and cold drinks. The time when I had grown breasts, still not full like Mama's but quite nice, and Terry held them and sucked the nipple and put his finger in my hole at the donga we kids roofed over with branches as our headquarters in the veld. His name was Tertius, teacher told us it means number three, but he was first-born, we used to tease him, his parents were stupid. I was in junior choir at our church, with Mama in the ladies' choir. Daddy—oh he had me with him so many times, we went to watch dirt-track racing, very exciting, and when there was a fun fair set up in our township and a circus he bought tickets for us for the rides and the seats. He held my hand when I was scared that the lion was going to bite the tamer. When I was little I used to climb into their big bed between them and cuddle on Sunday mornings, and when I grew bigger and didn't anymore they didn't know about Terry and the headquarters we kids had.

Then—without a death yet, without the proper end—that Return ended. There was Miss Denise Appolis, trainee at the bank. Now it comes to me in English. I live in a flat in the city with another girl. We're white—well of course, what else could we be? What a question. Like other people who work in the bank or the attorney's office where my friend is also some sort of trainee. We try out different hairstyles together, have boyfriends we mock and laugh about when we're alone, we go to parties. But sometimes this Denise Appolis who I am goes, crosses from one self to another, to a place and people, feelings towards these people, that should belong to another Return entirely. So I don't know what happened to the force that sends me back, again and again, but never as the same being, even if, rarely, I do have a recognition that must come from another life. How can there be two in one Return?

There are no answers.

There is no answer. Only that you have to go back, in whatever form, again and again.

Perhaps there are things people on the planet decree upon one another that would explain this freak Return that once happened.

'I have been part of it always and there is maybe no escape, forgetting and returning life after life like an insect in the grass.'

I would have been Denis—if she hadn't pushed her way into the world first. They were expecting me. Hoped for, planned for—a son. So far as you could then; it was before the discovery of tests that would reveal the sex of what was in the womb. They knew only that we were two of us—Gemini—in the biological package.

Still-born. Which means you don't get a name. Still-born: means 'still' in the sense of unable to breathe, to move, to live. So it's true that my corporeal life outside the shelter, the womb, was only the passage from the birth canal to the hospital incinerator. You have seen a foetus? Head and genitals—that's it. Both out-size. What is inbetween is dismissable. Because a foetus doesn't have to eat, digest, evacuate. Head and genitals—intelligence and sex. That's about what I was; she had hogged the vital juices meant for both of us and she emerged ready to meet the re-quirements, fully formed. I was the runt, underdeveloped, the feeble heart arrested, not even incubator material, still-born. Never got further than that. Only head and genitals, intelligence and sex as my share of experiencing the world in the flesh the way *you* do; but never to have your experience of humiliating functions that, from the tangled nuisance of gut and stuff, plague and disrupt these two great powers! You begin to understand? I wonder . . .

Memory belongs to the corporeal—you have to have lived, to travel your time through the body, to remember. I have no memory of my own beyond that passage from the birth canal to the incinerator. Instead I find I flit about, I experience snatches of corporeal life of any and all of you, as I please. That's the explanation for my non-existent existence. Of which I have proof to offer in response to your disbelief.

How is it that I think? Know words? Something of history, literature, politics, contemporary life, what it's all like—as you'll see. Is it the collective unconscious some of you believe in, others deride? Or do I have, as the ancient religious mystics believed and some of your fashionable novelists resort to for their characters, in invigoration of flagging invention—the ability to inhabit someone's body, invade his or her experience as incubus, succubus, dybbuk—I don't know. But I do no harm; the subject isn't even aware of what I have appropriated and is not deprived in any way; there's enough for both of us. You'd be surprised if you knew how much goes to waste in your experience; how much you don't grasp, just don't get it, don't (what's your word) intuit, and how much you don't want to accept, although it's been provided.

And even that faculty of memory, which as I've told you, I don't have because I've lived nothing to remember except that trip from the birth canal to the incinerator you're tired of hearing about—you, with your corporeal ability to create memories, don't always retain the ability to hold on to them, and that can be either your kind of deprivation or your protection against the suffering I see you're subject to in the stages of mortality. There's

an old man I know *in my way*, whose occupation of your kind of
life is the same chair each day and whose corporeal activity is
moving between it and the bathroom on a contraption like one
I've seen infants supporting themselves on as they are learning to
walk. He was a scaler of mountains and once was part of an
Everest expedition that if it did not reach the summit gallantly
survived an attempt in dangerous weather conditions; friends
and even an occasional journalist come to talk to him about this,
and while he smiles with pleasure to be reminded that it must
have been an experience somewhere in the past that has abandoned him, he cannot relive any moment of it. The friends and
the journalists find this sad; it depresses them and I'm the one
who knows why, because while I'm living their experience *I* accept the meaning within them they suppress: living is growing
old on the way to death, losing those faculties they treasure so
much, and although they think their lives are choices, there are
the two stages over which they don't have any choice—to be
born, and to die.

But when I'm experiencing the old man I reach into something else laid away in his past to which he no longer has access.
He dearly loves his wife (feeling this, with my own precocious, arrested awareness of sexuality, those genitals I was at least equipped
with, I have an inkling of what I've missed, the joy *she*, my
greedy twin, robbed me of as she shouldered me aside). The wife
is much younger than the old man, she lies beside him and the
life that is in her keeps him going, she buries her warm face in
the grave between his jaw and skeletal shoulder-blade. She is the
joy I experience in him and he's going to die happy because he
does not remember the long love affair she had with another
man, in the middle years of their marriage, which caused him

such violent misery and demeaning jealousy, and almost—
imagine that, since he possesses her totally now—led him to divorce her.

. And she? Isn't that female lucky? Not merely *forgiven*, if you
please! It never happened. The cheat never lied. The bitch never
came home and sat at dinner with another man's semen inside
her. But don't be too sure about her. I know in her that other
something I'll never have: remorse. In her chest there's a tight-
ening as if a drawstring has pulled together all that she did, that
time, there's an emotional congestion she can't relieve by asking,
as she longs to, his forgiveness. For what? he would say, lovingly.
For what, my darling? And to remind him would be the final
cruelty of all she did to him.

But there's even more to it. The complexity of these lives of
yours between birth and death! I wake up as her in the night and
she raises herself to listen for his breathing. Her love for him is
devastating. She has never contemplated death but now knows
sorrow will be silence.

And how does *she* live, that sister who twinned my life with
hers in the closest meaning of the word, worse than any freakish
Siamese twinning, for she grabbed the chance, the oxygen, at
any cost. Does she live it up, doubly, for both of us who fought
it out in the womb? The odd thing is, I can't take on, as I do here
and there, as the fancy moves me, her consciousness and subconscious. I have difficulty even in identifying her. I can't find
her. Sometimes I think I'm on the wave-length . . . but it's just a
choking exclamation that strangles. It's the umbilical cord that
was round my neck. Never mind her; how would I have lived—
quite unlike her, for sure, however her way might have turned
out to be. I can't pretend to be without prejudice; I can't imag-

ine, in the here-and-there of the lives I light upon, anything particularly interesting or fulfilling for her. I don't think she merits it. But I should like to experience her, to confirm this. Although I would have been a man (evidence that outsize bunch between the legs of the wretched little corpse) if I had not been still-born, my disembodied state, as you've no doubt noticed, means that I can enter both male and female experience—in my own way.

Don't think it's all grave. (No pun intended.) Only now— what you would call a little while ago, or a day ago, in your measuring-out of your time—I was on a bicycle with curved handles like the horns of some swift beast. The bicycle and I were cutting a swathe through the air up a tree-lined street. Gateways, houses, telephone poles sliced away from us on either side, leaves and branches rushed out to meet—and just missed—us. On my head was a yellow casque slashed with red arrows. I had eyes that could see as keenly as fish in the depths of an ocean. I had a heart: I was that pump, a creature whose corporeality was all one pulse of energy. Glory. Mouth open to gulf wild laughter. Whoever you were, half-grown boy: I understood from you what it means to be alive!

Glory.

Some I've come upon can't find it simply, as the boy did, in this life that you complain about continually yet cling to fiercely—even abjectly, as I've come to know, in circumstances you yourselves bring about. Like ticks on the body of the world, you suck there inert until you bloat and fall off. Ugh.

Glory: there are others—completely other. They believe it can't be experienced in corporeality, it belongs to something they visualize: an after-life. Which must be the opposite term of stillborn (you can tell I hang around intellectuals and amateur philosophers). Perhaps that's where I belong, if anywhere: their after-life, because I've missed out what's inbetween. How do they get to their after-life? Strapped to the chest of that other being I took on—hardly older than the bicycle rider, he must have been—was a device with a stopper like a heavy pin. The thing was hard against the breast-bone under a flowing garment; on the crown of the head I was also aware of an embroidered skull-cap. The pin came out with an easy tug. There was an embrace more passionate than any I've been privy to, and without boasting, I don't mind telling you there've been quite a few, between men-and-men and women-and-women, as well as the kind of woman-man one that half-created me. This one was between man and man and the climax was an orgasm unlike any other, unsurpassable, an explosion that ended everything, for both. There was nothing to remember of it, for him, my chosen partner, just as for myself, who can only borrow memory. I don't know if the Believer I was, for a while, for the flashed duration of the embrace, received the reward of the after-life, and if it was better than the one that flew apart in darkness beyond any dark. I left him at that moment of nothingness. *You* will perhaps know because *you* will have lived, whereas I have never existed in my own right, and if you don't experience life you don't experience its end. I suppose I could go on the way I do for ever, while you, my friend, you will come to that nothingness one way or another, in bed slowly or fast on a highway, even if it is extremely unlikely that anyone would find reason to bring you into a final clinch with a grenade.

The victim for whose last embrace I was decisive was, of course, a political leader. I don't make moral judgments, despite the bits and ends of theoretical justice I've picked up, so I don't know if he had it coming to him. And if he did, did he deserve it? There's not enough sequence in my fragments of experience to judge what I'll risk as the most important question for you: does killing really solve any of the conflicts between you, and what you claim as your countries, your boundaries? I mean, you can't turn me away at Immigration, so how can I presume to know what cans you like a commodity, contains your individual experience as imprinted within you from the day you're born Here or There rather than Somewhere Else.

My dipping into the experience of politicians has resulted in some discoveries you probably wouldn't credit, considering the general view of these individuals I overhear. They are stalwart, convinced of their moral right to take power, determined to bring peace, prosperity and justice to all, if you are of those who support their ideas of how a government should run your lives; they are ruthless, power-hungry, wily, will stop at no infamy to impose their kind of regime, if you are in opposition to their ideas of governing you. In the being of one—a politician—once in a while (there are so many buzzing around among you, how could I avoid the temptation or the curiosity) I have known the raw surface of weakness (yes) to any failure, however small, any setback to high self-esteem, however temporary, they conceal from public sight. While they are declaring themselves satisfied with the support they are gaining among the collective electorate—You—the loss of a few votes is to them a slow bleeding from some secret organ they have, the loss of a seat in the palace of government is a lopping-off of a limb of the creature they have to make of themselves—for You, for your sake. You know that? Power is needed, there's a need to be *intact* for good, as well as for evil. I have some notion of those two concepts—come to me, in my way; how could I have even the most fleeting contacts with your experience without finding out that they actually do exist.

Perhaps I would have been one of those, a politician. Because I can't keep away from them, they attract me with the strong sense with which they wrestle life, the secrecy of the holds they use, under the public surface; their kind of survival tactics among the different ones I see practised among you, from withdrawals to the ashram to the total exposure of the pop star. Why shouldn't I try them all, since I don't have the angst of going through the whole way with any! But no. If I imagine a corporeal life for myself—what Denis might be—maybe I would have been a writer; fiction, of course, because that's the closest a corporeal being can get to my knack of living other lives; multiple existences that are not the poor little opportunities of a single existence.

When *she* dies—the one who precociously stole my life, I'd like to know how much value she's added to it on your stock market—I wonder whether my non-existent existence will stop, too: still-born to stop-dead. I doubt it. I'm curious, nevertheless. So one of the favourite diversions of my eternity is to board a plane in the being of a passenger. Because I find the nearest you who are not religious—can't rely on an after-life—may get to experience the eternal is up at around thirty thousand feet on the way to the heaven of those who believe they're going to go all the way. In a layer of the atmosphere outside the earth, between time-zones defined by your earthly existence: you don't know precisely, up above the earth's cloud-shroud, its cosy blanket, whether you are X hours behind or X hours ahead of the earthly destination you have headed yourself for. So you are out of both time and place—precariously? No—you inhabit both at the same time, clouds, space, and the interior box of the aircraft, which is like a hospital ward, you are designated to yours (First, Business, Tourist class), your bed (seat number) and you are dependent on the ministrations of the nurse (cabin attendant). Freedom is just beyond the window; as always with you, you can see it but can't touch it. And it is fearful . . .

So I am everybody's twin?—oh no, no, not at all! Don't mistake me. Not in anything I've said. I'm not an *alter ego, doppelgänger*, clone—nobody's alternate. I am not stopping up your ears with a homily on universality, living human beings are part of one another, must love one another etcetera, with my wine-tastings of your experience here-and-there as the high-minded symbolic lesson. In my condition I have no moral responsibility. Now do you get it? How could I when I don't have to *provide*: don't have to eat, to have a roof over me, don't have to look over my shoulder at anyone who's a rival in acquisitions? It's easy for me . . .

I suppose, in the end, you have to be disembodied, like me, to need no morals. All that I have in common with you is *all you are not*—I am. Pity me. Or envy me.

'It turns out that something that never was and never will be is all that we have.'

For so long—well, the ten years we've been together—we've had everything we wanted. Not some gift from the gods or nice middle-class family inheritance, but in the independent making of our own lives. Karen is overseas investment advisor of the most successful group of brokers in the city. I had a history of having been an activist. That cliché means I was part of actions against the old regime, now put away mummified if not exactly returned to dust, that got me tear-gassed and beaten-up and once detained—another cliché, this one for a spell inside without trial. But I am a lawyer who nevertheless managed to get herself accepted, in a renewed country, as fresh blood and a woman, by one of the most prestigious old legal practices. So that's the career side of it.

As women who've wanted and had only women lovers since youthful attempts with men, we know we were lucky—extraordinarily blessed—to find one another. Even straight people (as they think of themselves) prove how rare the right relationship is: divorces, remarriages, quarrels over child custody—anyway, that's the mess we've freed ourselves of, in what's called our sexual preference. Which has been and is open, since the law now accepts its existence as legitimate and we both have the confidence of our recognised career capabilities and loving sexual partnership (the straight couples enviously see how fulfilling it is) to ignore any relics of old prejudice that turn up in long-faced disapproval. We find the society of our own kind naturally compatible, with the usual rivalries, of course, haphazard sexual attractions that complicate and trouble, not too seriously, everyone's social life, golf club or gay bar. But we also have heterosexual friendships, particularly those coming about through our different professional connections, and we don't mind obliging as the female dinner-partners of visiting overseas businessmen or other dignitaries who have arrived without spouses. Karen is something of a beauty with the added advantage or disadvantage of being younger than I am, and she sometimes is pursued by one of these men-of-passage after the occasion, and I suppose I must admit that it pleases, rouses me to know that my lover appeals to someone who can't have her, whom she would reject. With the funny little pursed-up, half-derisive, half-flattered face she makes as we look the man over in retrospect.

We bought a house two years after we met, and one of ours, an architect friend, renovated it to create exactly what we think our place ought to be. The mixed-media paintings and the one or two sculptures (we like wood and can't stand the pretension of *objets trouvés*) are the work of other artist friends. Our collection and our travels together are what we enjoy spending our money on. We've seen a good part of the world (four eyes better than two), the Great Wall, the Barrier Reef, New York–Chicago–West Coast, Kyoto, Scottish Highlands, Florence-Rome-Paris—and there'll be a lot more to come, but it's always with an emotional dissolve of pleasure, arms going about each other, that we find our two selves back—home. I've had the impression that straights don't believe such a concept should exist, with us. Because we don't deserve it, eh.

Some time last year something surprising—yes, happened. Not to us; but came from us. Not surprising, though, that it occurred at the same time in both, as our emotions, concepts, opinions and tastes are non-biological identical twins. For instance, I don't know whether, talking with others, we're heard to say 'I' instead of 'we'. The totally unexpected thing—if that's what surprise is—is that this one was, well, biological. How else could you term it. We wanted to have a child. I'm sure—and I use the singular personal pronoun for once because we never actually expressed this, I'm observing from some imagined outside—we were aware that the desire was like the remnant of a tail, the coccyx, vestigial not of our human origin as primates but of the family organism we have evolved beyond. But freedom means you go out to get what you want, even if it seems its own contradiction. Reject the elements of family and take one of them to create a new form of relationship.

We have a home to offer, no question about that, vis-à-vis the basic needs of a child. It's the first consideration an agency would take account of: this easily, informally beautiful place and space we've created. But adoption is not what we want: we're talking of our own child. This means one of us must bear it, because what one is the agency of becomes the possession of both.

Late at night, accompanied by the crickets out on the terrace, later still, in our bed, her arm under my head or mine under hers, we consider how we're going to go about this extraordinary decision that seems to have been made for us, not at all like the sort of mutual decision, say, to go to the Galápagos next summer instead of Spain. There's no question of who will grow the child inside her body. Karen is eight years younger than I am. But at thirty-six she has doubts of whether she can conceive. —How do I know? I've never been pregnant.— We laughed so much I had to kiss her to put a stop to it. She hasn't had a man since at eighteen in her first year at university her virginity was disposed of, luckily without issue, by a fellow student in the back of his car. —I think there are tests you can have to see if you're fertile. We'll find a gynecologist. None of her business why you want to know.—

That was simple. She's fertile, all right, though the doctor did make some remark about the just possible difficulties—did she say complications, Karen doesn't remember—for (what did she call her) a *primapara* at thirty-six, and the infant. There's always a caesarian—but I don't want Karen cut up. —I'll have a natural birth, I'll do all the exercises and get into the right frame of mind these prenatal places teach.— And so we know, I know now; she's going to have an experience I won't have, she's accepted that; we've accepted that, yes.

But then comes the real question we've been avoiding. This is a situation, brought upon by ourselves indeed, where you can't do without a man. Not yet; science is busy with other ways to fertilise the egg with some genetically-programmed artificial invader, but it's not quite achieved.

The conception.

We think about that final decision, silently and aloud. The decision to make life, that's it, no evasion of the fact.

—There's—well. One of the men we know.—

What does Karen mean. I looked at her, a stare to read her. I can't bear the idea of a man entering Karen's body. Depositing something there in the tender secret passage I enter in my own ways. Surely Karen can't bear it either. Unfaithful and with a man.

Karen is blatantly practical. I should be ashamed to doubt her for an instant. —Of course he could produce his own sperm.—

—Milk himself.—

—I don't know—a doctor's rooms, a lab, and then it would be like an ordinary injection, for me. Almost.—

—Someone who'd do it for us. We'd have to look for . . . choose one healthy, good-looking, not neurotic. Do we know anyone among our male friends who's all three?—

And again we're laughing. I have a suggestion, Karen comes up with another, even less suitable candidate. It's amazing, when you're free to make a life decision without copulation, what power this is! You can laugh and ponder seriously, at the same time.

—We're assuming that if we select whoever-it-is he's going to agree, just like that.—

I didn't know the answer.

—Why should he?—

Karen's insistence brought to mind something going far beyond the obliging male's compliance (we could both think, finally, that there would be one or two among our male friends or acquaintances who might be intrigued by the idea). What if the child turned out to look like him. More than a resemblance, more than just common maleness if it were to be a boy, more than something recognisably akin to the donator of the sperm, if a girl. And further, further—

—Oh my god. If the child looks like him—even if it

doesn't—he gets it into his head to claim it. He wants, what's the legal term you use in divorce cases, you know it—access. He wants to turn up every Sunday to have his share, taking the child to the zoo.—

We went for long walks, we went to the theatre and to the bar where we girls gather, all the time with an attention deep under our attention to where we were and what we were hearing, saying. Conception. How to make this life for ourselves.

After a week, days clearing of thinning cloud, it became simple; had been there from the beginning. The sperm bank. This meant we had to go to a doctor in our set and tell what we hadn't told anybody: we want a child. Karen is going to produce it. We don't wish to hear any opinions for or against this decision that's already made, cannot be changed. We just need to know how one approaches a sperm bank and whether you, one of *us*, will perform the simple process of insemination. That's all. Amazement and passionate curiosity remodelled the doctor's face but she controlled the urge to question or comment, beyond saying I'm sure you know what it is you're doing. She would make the necessary arrangements; there would be some payment to be made, maybe papers to sign, all confidential. Neither donor nor recipient will know that the other exists.

The whole process of making a life turns out to be even blinder than nature. Just a matter of waiting for the right period in Karen's cycle when the egg is ready for the drop of liquid. Anonymous drop.

And waiting, unnecessarily looking at the calendar to make sure—waiting is a dangerous state; something else came to life in us. Karen was the first to speak.

—From the lab, the only way. But who will know if it's from a white? Or a black? Can one ask?—

—Maybe. Yes. I don't know.—

But after the moment of a deep breath held between us, I had to speak again, our honesty is precious. —Even if the answer's yes, how can we be sure. Bottled in a laboratory what goes into which?—

The sperm of Mr Anonymous White Man. Think what's in the genes from the past, in this country. What could be. The past's too near. They're alive, around—selling, donating?—their seed. The torturers who held people's heads under water, strung them up by the hands, shot a child as he approached; the stinking cell where I was detained for nine weeks, although what happened to me was nothing compared with all the rest.

If the anonymous drop contains a black's DNA, genes? It would bring to life again in Karen's body, our bodies as one, something of those whose heads were held under water, who were strung up by the hands, a child who was shot. No matter whether this one also brings the contradictions of trouble and joys that are expected of any child.

But how can one be sure? Of that drop?

We keep talking; our silences are a continuation. Shall we take the risk. How would we know, find out? Years, or perhaps when he, the white child, is still young; you see certain traits of aggression, of cruel detachment in young children—the biological parents ask, where did he get it from, certainly not from you or me. When he—the child we're about to make somehow is thought of now as a male—is adolescent, what in the DNA, the genes, could begin to surface from the past?

We postponed. We went to the Galápagos, perspective of another world. Now that we're back we don't talk about making a life, it is not in our silences—home, alone, as it was before.

So I was never born. Refused, this time. I suspect it was the only time. But then what I have is not what is experienced as memory.

'Just as everything is always something else . . . it may also throw some light on the procreative god.'

The Germans know they are losing. It is after the war of bombs falling on cities. In our family we stayed alive through all that. We Russian bears, we've come into the fight on the other side, we're going to win for the English and French who can't do it for themselves. While the final battles go on at the front the Germans still occupy our old city, but only just. We have our people who move around in the streets we know so well and knife them at night. So they come to our houses with their guns and frighten the women, smashing the furniture and throwing out whatever's in cupboards and under beds, while they search for our men they know do these things. They shout all the time so loud, like a stampeding herd of cattle through the house, that I can hardly hear my sisters screaming and I don't know what my mother, her mouth wide over tight teeth, is trying to tell me to do. Run? How could I get away. They took my father, kicking him to our door, well at least we know that he had managed to get back at them before they got to him, he killed at least three in the times he left us at night and crept back into bed beside my mother before light. Then one of them looks round; and takes me. Kicks me after my father. My mother howls at them, He's only fourteen, a baby, he knows nothing, nothing! But they don't understand Russian. Anyway, they know

that soon when I'm fifteen I'll be called up, there are boys
from my class who are now in our army because we must win,
everyone must fight. They throw my father and me into a kind
of military van and keep us on the floor with their feet on us but
I see the tops of buildings near our street go past and the towers
of the old church my mother goes to and says it was built centuries ago and is the most beautiful in our country, in the world,
and it was God who spared it from the bombing. And I even
see the one wall, sticking up, of the theatre that was bombed,
where we once went to see my eldest sister, she's an actress, play
a part in a play by Maxim Gorky. We'd also read it in my class
at school.

Seeing these things, still there, I can't believe I'm here so
scared I can hardly breathe. My father keeps trying to turn his
head to look at me, I know he wants to tell me it's all right, he's
with me.

Then there are tops of buildings I don't know, and then no
buildings, only sky. My nose is running. No, I'm crying! Baby! I
snort the tears back up through my nose, my father mustn't
know.

We get wherever it is they're taking us and the army van
opens in a yard, very bright high lights like in a sports field but
there's a building with bars at the windows. They take my father
away but not to the building and I call, I yell, but they don't let
him answer, I see his shoulders struggling. The Germans who're
holding me take me into the building. It's a prison. I've only seen
the inside of a prison in films. There's some argument going on,
I don't understand their language but I think it's because they
don't know what to do with me.

I know they're going to shoot my father. This fear that takes away the movement of my legs, the Germans are holding me up, dragging me along passages, is it fear for him or for me. But why don't they take me away to be shot wherever they're doing it to him. They open an iron door and throw me into a small place, dark, with a square of light cut by thick black bars. When they have gone I make out that there's nobody but me and a patch that must be a blanket.

I've been here days now, they bring me water and food sometimes and there's a bucket that stinks of me. But it's as if nothing ever happened to me, I am not Kostya who was in school and played second league football and went shopping to carry for my mother and had already invited Natalya to the cinema, paying for her, there is only the ride on the floor of the military van beside my father, and the church tower and the theatre wall sticking up, and his back as he went to be shot. Because if he wasn't shot he would be in this place with me. We would be very close because this space is very small, there's hardly room to spread the blanket to lie down. There's a wall in my face whichever way I turn. If I jump with my hands ready I can just reach and grab the iron bars on the bit of window and hang there. But it's difficult to haul up my head and shoulders so I can see anything. Only the bars. I feel the bars in my hands, if I lie on the blanket and close my eyes, I see the bars. Sometimes I have the crazy idea that my head is getting smaller, if I can think it into getting small enough I could stick it through the bars. My head would be out of the tight walls, the bars wouldn't be there on my eyes even when my eyes are closed.

What can they do with me? They can't send me back home

to tell everyone everything. They've lost the war. There they are at the door, they leave it open a moment, stare at me. A loud word in their language. They've come.

Taking me away to be shot. The bars still there on my eyes.

'The Pestle of the moon
That pounds up all anew
Brings me to birth again—
To find what once I had,
And know what once I have known.'

The grandmother used to talk about the war and after the war when there were plans in which the government would build up everything that was lost and the man with the great moustache was power in the world just like the American president and she had been on a trip with a women's group to Moscow to see the other one in his tomb, dead but still as if he was alive among everyone in the country. The granddaughter was born after the one with the great moustache was also dead and she grew up under the public display of portraits of those, one by one, who came after him; successive faces of the father she didn't have. Apparently he had left her mother for another woman when his child was too small to have kept memory of him. The Government fathers provided good schools and clinics for children, and her mother had a steady job in a catering business, conditions for whose employees were ensured by their trade union. The grandmother had her pension.

The child was taken with her school class (like her grand-mother's group, earlier, but not to the tomb) to museums and the overawing, dwarfing interiors of splendid buildings which had survived the war and been restored, palaces and theatres from way back in the history of Czars, now belonging, the Government said, to the people. She loved these expeditions; the chipped but glorious gilt, bulbous cupolas, flying crenellated arrows of spires aimed at the clouds, the saints painted in deserted chapels—religion was not taught in schools, and only the very old, like her grandmother, ventured to go and pray in museum-churches without priests to receive them. God was not there. But the grandmother privately could not accept this: that he did not exist. The young girl introduced her mother to the splen-dour that belonged to the city of their unchanging routine of school, work, food queues, and when the State ballet came on tour, they went together to be dazed with enchantment—tickets were cheap, ordinary workers could afford such pleasures. She had decided she wanted to be a teacher; and then, seeing com-puters working magically in television shows, changed to the ambition to learn computer skills and maybe work in a regional Government office. Her mother's trade union would know how the daughter should go about this, when the time came.

But when the time came, she had completed her school edu-cation, it was a different time. Another time. The great fathers lost power, lost hold, the countries that had made a vast union under one name, broke apart. The intellectuals and others the fathers had feared and imprisoned were let out. The world out-side told, now all would be free. Bring the computers, bring the casinos, bring whatever the West says that makes happiness that we've never tried, couldn't have. And they did. And the new Government that had never done business the West's way didn't do well, now in business with them.

Factories closed without the market for their products that had existed conveniently in the vast union. Elena's mother lost her job when the catering firm failed in competition with what were called fast-food chains with American names which replaced many restaurants, Elena could not study to become a teacher or a computer operator. She had to find work, any work. Foreigners come to do business lived in hotels refurbished, by the international chains that had taken them over, to make them feel they were in an hotel in the West. Her mother could not believe it: her daughter, so clever, who was going to make a career in that very world, the new world, came home one day to tell that she had found work: as a chambermaid in one of the hotels. She was instructed to wear a skirt, not jeans, and supplied with a uniform apron. She passed doors hung with the sign 'Do Not Disturb' in English, French, German and Japanese, and knocked softly on others. If there was no response, she was to go in, make the beds, vacuum the carpets, clean the bathroom, replace the towels, soap and whatever was missing from the basket of free miniatures of bath-oil, shampoo, provided in the high cost (payable in dollars only) of the room. The sheets were stained with semen. The drain-traps of the bathtubs were blocked with pubic hairs. The lavatory bowls often were not flushed of traces of shit. Socks stiff with sweat and shirts dirty at collar and cuffs had to be picked up off the carpet and placed neatly on a chair. The housekeeper came regularly to see if such things were correctly done.

Sometimes when the chambermaid knocked there was no re-

ply and she went in, there was someone there, a voice from under the shower, and she would apologise and leave at once. There
were times when she entered after no reply and a man was standing, half-dressed, and while she apologised he would smile and
say, go ahead, I've finished with the bathroom. But she had her
instructions: I'll come back later. There was the morning when
she knocked and someone answered in a language she didn't
recognise as English (learnt a little at school), German, French or
Japanese. She turned away but the door opened and a man in the
white towelling dressinggown the hotel provided in the bath-
rooms blocked the light of the room. —No Italian?—okay, understand English? Come please.— She followed him to the
bathroom and he pointed to the bathtowels that had fallen from
their rail into the water. She signalled: I bring some more. When
she came back with the towels he thanked her, smiling, shrug-
ging effusively at the good service, —You Russian? Yes, I'm sure
you're real Russian girl. First one I know!— She smiled back as a
maid should, polite to a guest, never mind their dirt. Nodded
determinedly. —Russian, yes.— She said it in her language, and
he cocked his head a little as if hearing a bird call. They both
laughed, and she left. Next day when she knocked at 507 the
door opened at once. He was a large man, the Italian, tall and
broad but not fat, with a fancy belt that still met above a strong
belly, and a fresh full face, black thick-lidded eyes, and a glossy
crest of grey hair worn consciously as a cock his comb. The age
of many of the foreign guests, somewhere at the end of the
fifties. She saw all this, really, for the first time: he was present-
ing himself.

Again he signalled her into the room. He had unpacked
some purchase; there was a jumble of cardboard box, bubble

wrap, plastic chips. Could she do something about this mess? They communicated well by signs and their few English words, her willingness, his appreciation brought laughter. He helped her gather the pieces from the carpet, fill the box, picked it up and made to carry it to the door for her, while she protested, trying to take it from him. It fell and spilled again. He threw his hands above his head in mock culpability. When they came down again they went round her, he was rocking her against him, laughing. She pulled away. He let her go. —Don't be cross. Come sit down.— She did not know what she was supposed to do. You must not be rude to a hotel guest. He sat on the velvet chaise-longue and patted the place beside him. She came slowly to the summons. Now he put his one arm round her shoulders and turned her to him, kissed her. His lips were warm and pleasant, a change from the dirt she associated with hotel guests, he smelled of pine aftershave. He pressed her closer and put his tongue in her mouth. The caress, the advances came from that other world, outside, the world of computers and travel, even while she resented what he was doing, it took her there, away from the chambermaid.

He was waiting, every morning. He would be in the dressinggown at his laptop computer or on the telephone, surrounded by a calculator, another—a mobile—phone and spread documents. She could see he was a big businessman of some kind. This was the equipment they all had in their rooms. He would gesture her to him and run a free hand down her buttocks while he argued, agreed, lowered his voice confidentially, raised it confidently in Italian. Business over, he made love to her on the bed she would make up afresh in the course of her work, later.

She had been clumsily penetrated by a youth who ejaculated halfway but she did not know the act could be like this. The entry of this man was an exquisite opening up of all that must have been secret inside her and when some sort of flame jetted from his strong movements within the sheath he wore she was lit up all through her body down her shuddering thighs and he had to shush her cry—there might someone passing in the hotel corridor.

She had her rooms to clean; he had his appointments to meet. He found a better arrangement: what was her lunch-hour? He would arrange his meetings accordingly, his business lunches could be scheduled late. Between embraces he would feed her cherries and slices of peach from the bowl the hotel kept replenished on his coffee table, poor little girl, no time for her to lunch.

His stay at the hotel was longer than usual for foreign businessmen; he must have had complex financial deals that meant waiting for the opportunity to make this connection or that with an intermediary. She was told nothing of this, or anything else about his life where he came from, Italy, but she saw how he was often exasperated when he put down the telephone or grew impatient with the fax facility attached to it. The third week, must have been—one lunchtime he looked at her lying under him, rising on his elbows for a better perspective. His mouth shaped and reshaped as if he were urging himself to make some gesture not physical, toward what it was time to leave behind: pleasures dictating one course, judgment the other. When she was dressing he watched her. That responsive body concealing itself; he had had many responsive bodies coming and going in his life, but time was passing and one more . . .

—I can take you to Italy.—

She didn't believe him, didn't answer.

—No, it's true. I know someone, I can get you papers. We'll find work for you there. Not this, here. Better work. You can't go on in this place.—

She shook her head, lower and lower. He was smiling, dismissing her powerlessness before his capability in the world of official fixes.

What could he know of the mother, the grandmother she went back to every night with leftover food one of the chefs smuggled from the hotel restaurant to give her.

—First days of next month, I go. I take you. Nothing for a girl like you, here.— Every lunchtime he confirmed, assumed the arrangement. And she found her voice: —No, no I cannot.—

At last he lost interest—all right. There were plenty of girls who would jump at the chance to get out. And there are plenty of girls in Milan even if they haven't the novelty of being a real Russian one.

But when she was walking home from the bus stop on her afternoon off duty she saw something so terrible that she was almost run over by a truck as she plunged across the traffic to reach it. Old people begging in the streets; they were everywhere, old men in the remnants of their respectable functionaries' or clerks' suits, old women with the bewildered faces of former housewives, shamed under shawls. But this one she was in panic to reach was her own grandmother. She took her home, unable to speak, eyes screwed with tears of anger, disgust, as if the old woman were a criminal caught in the act. At home, her mother first cried and then countered with an anger of her own.

—She hasn't had her pension paid for a year—one month more than a year. I stand with her for days outside the office, no-one is paid. What can they do but sit in the street and hope someone has something to give? Why shouldn't she do what they do? How can we live on what you bring from that hotel? I'll have to try and put her in an old people's home, she'll die there away from us! What else is there?— Next day the grandmother was back on her stool in the street. Her granddaughter saw her, and passed.

There was something else.

After the lunchtime love-making she brought up the subject he had set aside. —If you can do papers, I go to Italy.—

It was not just the sight of the revered old woman begging in the street; the sometime chambermaid had something of the rational intelligence, calculation, of the businessman. He would find decent work for her in that country outside, Italy, that wonderful city he spoke about, Milan, and she would send good currency back to her mother. If she stayed a chambermaid her grandmother would remain a beggar among all the other beggars.

She left them behind. Her mother had not known about the Italian businessman but when told of his offer she did not hesitate: Go, Elena. They did not speak about what would become of those left behind. Perhaps the mother could take over the daughter's work as a chambermaid.

Her mother gave her in farewell a picture book of the city, its ancient palaces, churches, squares and museums they had visited together; she must have exchanged something for it in the market where people parted with their possessions, and the daughter herself asked for, and was granted, photographs taken in the city in times when her mother had a good position and they still owned a camera.

She had a room in a small hotel in his city, Milan, his country, Italy. The room was five floors up, a tiny cage of an elevator to take her there, bring him to her when he had time. The first day, he showed her a lacy stone spire just visible fretted out of the sky in the window. —You have a view of the Duomo! You must go to the piazza and see it, the most beautiful thing in the whole world.—

He paid for the hotel room and took her to a trattoria nearby where he had arranged with the patron for her to have her meals. It was a large and animated place where people working in the quarter came in a hurry to eat and drink plentifully. This was as he had told, a wonderful city; the narrow streets of shops displaying like art exhibitions beautiful clothes and shoes whose elegance you could not ever have imagined. He was looking out for something for her—work; but she had to have better clothes to wear if he should find that something! He took her to a department store that had good clothes on the racks, not as elegant as the small shops she gazed into, and bought for her trousers and jackets and shoes she had never had. Of course she always had been this tall, angular body with wide-apart breasts, this white skin and jutting cheekbones, shaggy dark hair, narrow black eyes and lips whose defining edges were attractively coarse in contrast with her skin; but now, in the shop mirror, she was seen by herself to be beautiful, in her way; as he, the Italian, must have seen her to be as a chambermaid. So she wandered the city dressed now like any of the smart working men and women from shops and offices, and hurried back to the hotel to see if there was any message from him; any day, every day, he might have found something, a job for her. She was listening avidly to the talk around her, reading the labels and signs on objects she could recognise, picking up a little of the language.

He did not come to claim love-making as often as he had back in that other hotel, her country. He had a great deal of work, a staff to direct, and she knew there was the apartment in some other part of the city where he lived with his wife; he had not talked about his family before he brought her to Italy, they couldn't talk much then or now because of their lack of a fluent common language, their tongues in love-making were the only real form of communication they had in common. But now he would mention that he wouldn't be coming to her from his offices next afternoon because his son had to be met at the airport or his wife was giving a cocktail party for her visiting relatives and he had to be home early. Although the city was a marvel surging around her she was more and more anxiously impatient to have work and belong to the city instead of being its spectator. Work and foreign currency to send back where she came from. And she also had the illusion—she knew it to be one—that she would pay him back, for the hotel, the trattoria, the clothes, in time; she would have liked the love-making not to be paid for in any way but the pleasure exchanged. But that, she knew, belonged to being in love. Men loved their wives. He loved his wife, she was sure of it, felt it; she had never had the chance to be in love.

He found something for her. And for himself as well.

It was not work, in Milan where he would be supposed to

keep coming to her—perhaps there was some new woman for that diversion, or his wife was getting suspicious and difficult. But he treated his women kindly and it so happened that a solution came up to benefit everybody, satisfy what he felt was his wide family responsibility, uncles, aunts, cousins, as well. He told her, one weekend (she did not usually expect him in those periods it was taken for granted he would spend with his wife and children), he wanted to introduce her to someone in his family. Perhaps there was an opportunity because the wife was away, or the relative was one with whom he exchanged confidences over affairs with women, someone to be counted upon to be discreet. But she was surprised and shyly touched at this sign of letting her into his life. After an hour's drive when the Alps were always present, approaching, withdrawing, as she followed this landscape that was Italy, the world, they came to a town, a large family apartment filled with imposing old dark furniture, generous food and wine laid out among the cries of people welcoming someone he told them he had saved from the chaos in Russia. They knew what a good man he was, generous. There was an aunt, another ample woman who might be her sister, a half-grown boy playing a computer game, the uncle, and a man who was the couple's son. The Russian stranger had observed, in Milan, how difficult it was to gauge the age of certain foreigners; they might look slim and briskly young seen from the back and turn age-seamed faces in which the bones of the nose were almost emerging from the thin skin, or they might appear to be well-fleshed, stout-muscled young men, thighs and buttocks stretching tight pants, the fleshy jaws and earlobes not necessarily giving away middle age. The son was one of these, and his mature vigour was the epicentre of the gathering. He had his own apartment; the Russian girl and the cousin from Milan who had brought her were taken by the man—Lorenzo, the name was, among all the names presented to her—to see his apartment almost as if there were a reason for this, such as an estate agent showing a prospective dwelling to a client.

There was a reason. The middle-aged son was not married; his parents did not know exactly why—there were a number of nice, goodlooking girls whose parents would have been only too pleased, lucky, to have a successful man with three butcher shops, two in town and another in a nearby village, as a son-in-law. There was some story of a love affair that had gone on for years with a married woman who wouldn't divorce; apparently it was over, she'd moved down south with her husband to Naples. Confidentially, the aunt and uncle in family council had told their worldly Milanese nephew to look out for a suitable wife from among the many women he must know, it was time for a man of Lorenzo's age and status to settle down. At the time, the Milanese nephew had raised high his eyebrows and pulled down his mouth; what city woman would want to come and live in a dull provincial town, among a few small factories and half-abandoned farms, nothing happening? But now there was a Russian girl he had brought from her wretched existence to his beautiful country out of kindness—yes, he fancied her for a while—and who would become a legal citizen by marriage to the son of one of the oldest families in a provincial town, what better solution to looking out for something for her! A well-off husband, every comfort, a man who could even afford to be generous and let her send money to her mother etc.—something she'd never have earned enough both to support herself and provide, by whatever humble work he might have found for her, a woman unable to speak the language, no qualifications but those of a chambermaid. He certainly wasn't going to pay her keep forever, and anyway the particular arrangements through which he'd made her entry possible had a time limit about to lapse.

Lorenzo came to Milan several times, something to do with a deal in hides, he tried to explain; he took her out to dinner in restaurants where the champagne bottles lolled in ice. He too, had a little English and praised her attempts at Italian, covering her hand with his in congratulation. He did not kiss her or make overtures to go to bed with her as she resignedly expected.

No, he was getting to know her. It had been proposed that she would be a suitable wife. She was an émigrée in doubtful legal standing, she was not in a position to decide whether she'd prefer to live in the city with the Duomo or in a small town, she had no prospects of a job other than to improve her Italian enough to sit at a comfortable desk and answer the telephone, greet customers as the wife of the owner in his high-class butcher shop—it would add to his local prestige to be shown to have settled down. And maybe even if the wife was a foreigner that would only evidence his superior flair in matters other than the way he prepared each customer's individual cut of meat with the skill and finesse of a surgeon.

Her Milanese came to her little hotel room with a view of the Duomo not to make love to her but to tell her that there was a great chance for her. The papers he had arranged for her in a certain way were no longer valid; she would be deported, nothing he could do about that. Lorenzo was ready to marry her. She would become an Italian wife, belong to this beautiful country. Lorenzo was a good man, not old, a man any woman would— he stopped, spread open his hands. Love; he didn't need to say it.

He came from Milan for the wedding. The aunt had been with her to a friend of the family who owned a shop in the town that was a modest version of the shops whose perfectly-composed windows made clothes works of art in the narrow streets of Milan; she had a wedding outfit and hat but not the girlish convention of white and long veil. The vigorous maturity of the bridegroom would have made this unsuitable; who knew what her background was, anyway, in that savage unknown vastness, Russia. They had not made love before the marriage, as if that was part of the arrangement. His love-making was concentrated, nightly regular as his butchering during the days. They couldn't talk much because of the language difficulty, again. There was no tenderness—but then she had not known any since that of her mother and grandmother towards her—but there was generosity: he insisted she buy herself whatever fine clothes she liked and presented her with jewellery, looking on at it with calculated pride, round her neck and on her wrists and fingers. Love-making between husband and wife was part of the rest of the days and nights, she went with him to his principal butcher shop in the morning, his customers who were all friends or long acquaintances of his family were introduced to her, smiled and congratulated her, lucky woman, and at night the couple came back to his apartment, cleaned and left in perfect order by a woman he could afford to employ daily. They lived on the primest of prime beef, cheeses and fruits exotic to her. She had never eaten so well in her life. In the first month of the marriage she was pregnant. He announced this to the whole family, his pride was theirs.

She brought out her picture book of her city, where she was conceived and born, where she was the child, and displayed the photographs taken when she and her mother visited the ancient churches (maybe they were the most beautiful in the world). How else can the stranger show she too has her worth—she hasn't come without a heritage. The husband's mother was enchanted; look, look, she thrust the book at his father, tried to distract her sister's adolescent grandson from his computer games. Lorenzo was again proud: so! His choice was not just some poor little foreigner from a frozen barbaric country ruined by communists, she had a provenance of ancient monuments, opera houses, churches, almost as Italy had her—unequalled, of course—treasures, which the family had never visited beyond those of Milan but knew of, owned by national right.

He wanted to show this woman, carrying his child, where he was born. Not in the town with his two butcher shops, where his parents had retired? No. No, the farm that had belonged to his great-grandfathers, grandfather and father. Now was his. Over a weekend extended by a religious holiday on a Monday—some saint's day or other—he was going to give her a treat there hadn't been the opportunity for in what was supposed to be their courtship. He would take her into the country to see his cattle farm developed from the old farm, source of his wealth, of the good life he provided for her. Another uncle and cousin run the operation for him, with their wives, in the old homestead he's renovated for them. Microwave, satellite TV—you'll see. The latest model installations, raising cattle for the supply of high quality beef he sold not only in his shops but supplied to supermarkets and restaurants in Milan, Turin and beyond.

She takes with her, shyly, knowing she won't be able to have much conversation with these relatives, either, the picture book and the photographs of the city she has had to leave behind. She puts on her gold bracelets and the necklace with an amber pendant (she'd chosen that because amber comes from her part of the world) which falls at the divide of her wide-apart breasts he appreciates so much.

It is a long drive—beautiful. Now and then she puts the flat of her palm on her stomach, she thought there was already a faint swell of the curve there; but really is amused at herself, all the prime meat they eat has made her less gaunt anyway. Whoever is in there—boy, girl—hasn't grown enough yet to make the presence evident. She is very well, no morning sickness his aunt had warned her of; a healthy Russian woman become an Italian wife. She feels a sudden—yes, happiness, it must be? At thirty, a new sense of life. As he drives, she looks from the landscape to this man dutifully received so weighty on top of her every night, with a recognition that he, too, must need this sense.

The old farmhouse shows its transformation to be his, as his gifts of fine clothes and jewellery transform her. When she uses the bathroom, it is all mirrors and flowered tiles. The new relatives embrace her, there is coffee and wine and cakes. Again the picture book and photographs go round; she summons her breathlessly hesitant words of their language to tell them the names of squares and churches, palaces. These glories that have survived are once more his wife's distinctions—she, his acquisition. He is gratified by the enthusiasm for Russia's old glory of these relatives who depend on him for their living: —You must go there one day.— In America it is said that people are booking trips to the moon . . .

Then it was time for the uncle and cousin to take her, led by her husband who owns it all, round the cattle-breeding installation. To her, cows graze in fields in summer, they are part of the green peace of a landscape as clouds are of a sky. There are brilliant fields stretching way behind the house. But no cows. There are sheds huge as aircraft hangars, and a great machine beside a solid wall of crushed maize that smells like beer.

Five hundred beasts. The owner knows his possessions exactly. In the hangars are five hundred beasts. The party is walked along the cement passage between each row, where the heavy heads face their exact counterparts on the opposite row. In front of each bowed head is a trough filled with the stuff that smells like beer. The huge eyes are convex blacked-out mirrors, expressing no life within. The broad, wet, black soft noses breathe softly upon the food. Some are eating; those that are not are in the same head-bowed position. They are chained by the leg. The bulk of each animal is contained—just—by the iron bars of a heavy stall; it cannot turn round. It can only eat, at this end of its body. Eat, eat. The butcher owner tells her: at six months, ready for slaughter. Prime.

Then she is led down the backs of the rows. Vast rumps, backsides touch the iron bars, hide streaked and plastered with the dung that falls into a trough like the one for food. The legs are stumps that function to hold up bulk.

She spoke only once—no need, the butcher owner keeps a running commentary of admiration of his beasts' condition, market prices. She puts together in English, out of the muddle of languages that inhibit her tongue: —When they go out in the fields?—

KARMA

Never. They spend the six months in the installation. That is the way meat production is done today. They are gelded—know what that is—he demonstrates. That's why they grow so fast and well!

She puts out a hand to touch the head above the shining eye-globes and the creature tries to draw away in fear but cannot move more than a few centimetres to either side, or front and back of the iron bars.

She turned from the men, absorbed in their talk and gestures, and walked out of the hangar looking only at the concrete under her feet. If the eyes followed her as she passed, she could do nothing for them. Nothing.

She stands outside, the sweetish beer smell from the wall of crushed maize in her nostrils as in theirs. She is swollen with such horror, her body feels the iron bars enclosing her, the bars are before her eyes, she cannot turn about, escape to the house. She does not know where it comes from, this knowledge—happening to her—of how it is for them, beasts born dumb as a human being can be made dumbly unable to free itself. It is as if that brief moment of awareness—happiness—had opened her to something in her she didn't, shouldn't know, a real memory she couldn't have had. There are many bad things endured in her abandoned, escaped life back—home—where the basilica from past centuries was world-renowned and her grandmother begged in the famous streets, her pension unpaid for years. But there is nothing, in her own record her life keeps, like this. And there is now, here, a child inside her seeded by the owner of these beasts in iron bars.

When the men come out, he takes her arm. —Tired?— And

231

to the other men, in their language —She's expecting, you know.— The news is repeated, over grappa, at the house. This aunt embraces her. There is a toast to the new addition soon to be welcomed in the family. A child with an inheritance—going to be born lucky.

She collected her picture book and photographs. At that moment she decided she would go there—home.

Back.

But to what?

Instead she found someone who, with the exchange of her few words, money, agreed to give her an abortion. And she told the butcher she had miscarried.

'The individual's choice of a future earthly body is limited, however . . .'

No. Whoever the interpreter was who wrote that was in ignorance. Choice? That's a temporal concept. There's no choice because choice implies a fixed personality to make it. I am an old being Returned in the being of a child; I find I'm back as a man, or Returned again to continue his experience in another time, place, as a woman. The gender is only one of the forms of Return. But if there can be any remnant of what I once really was—'really': how meaninglessly relative that is in so many, many Returns—it is the sense that I'm somehow more fully inhabited, as a male, than when the Return is female. And to carry over being from the earthly death of a young male to a woman, with the vestiges of what he endured inevitably continued somewhere in her—I inhabit her, I am her—that something in me of course becomes part of her, her personality her character as a being, although she doesn't know the reason.

And within her, a maleness I harbour resents this being—*hers*—as the victim she is in this phase of possible existences.

The first fish propelling itself by its fins over the slime to sand. That's when it all started.

They tell so.

And death: that's the end. Dead. They think I'm gone, but it's a process, lingering, between this past and that, lived. Can't call it memory? Something not even collective memory, because nobody comes back from the dead do they, to tell? I'm only some kind of answer—invented, dreamed into being?—to their awful fear of death everyone has from the beginning of earthly consciousness.

They think I'm disappearing, but always they're disappearing from me. Left behind. For this time.

I don't know in which Return I first heard about it. Read about it, it seems. I wish I never had. I believe if you don't know of some possibility, you'll never have to live it. Outside your orbit. Absurd, really, because I then must already have been a Return, the only *sure, actual* beginning is the fish—and even it had had a form of being in another element.

It must have been one of the Returns in which I had become middle-aged, even old—certainly adult, with a developed intellectual curiosity. Most times I was young, or a child. Short-lived:

at once available again. Must have been when I was a being dissatisfied with the explanations of human life on offer: given in churches, synagogues and mosques; or simply had the kind of restless mind that seeks out explanations in etymology and philosophical tracts and treatises. *'Karma. The sum and consequences of a person's actions during the successive phases of his existence, regarded as determining his destiny. Fate, destiny. Sanskrit* karman *(nominative* karma*), act, deed, work, from* karoti, *he makes, he does.'* The garble of the American Heritage Dictionary of the English Language. And there are other interpreters. *'The doctrine of* karma *or* transmigration . . . *is intimately associated with the philosophy of the Upanishads.'* I don't believe I ever read the Upanishads. Then there's: *'Officials, too, are subject to the laws of karma—that sooner or later every action brings its retribution, in this existence or in one to come.'* And another: *'. . . karma can be seen as the law of "eye for an eye and tooth for a tooth" . . . but such an interpretation is not only a simplification, but also a severe limitation.'*

Yes. Well, perhaps I don't understand and know I never shall what force sends me back to existence, but my experience doesn't bear out a process of either perfection or retribution. It has been written: *'Many people worry about the issues of "unfinished business" whether it be psychologically or karmically.'* The being I become to continue unfinished business in the life of another is not always, seldom is subject to any retribution owed by or to another life; and perfection's something I've never attained in a Return . . . This force I once heard, read about, they called karma—isn't it a *questioning* going back again and again? Here we are: *'Within such a search no single, narrow angle of perception is sufficient . . . From Hinduism and Buddhism; the doctrine that the sum of a person's actions in previous states of existence controls his or her fate in future existences.'* That's mostly been my existences. Even the one where I was—how to put it—waiting, was called back from existence I might have had.

After life.

The earthly term for what is hoped for after death. But here's a version of immortality for one who can't believe in an after-life somehow of a similar, if exalted, nature of the one they're living: when you die your body decays in earth or the process has been anticipated by cremation. Right? You are humus or ash; heat and rain, in the course of seasons cause the matter to rise in the form of evaporation and microscopic particles, to the atmosphere. It reconstitutes as clouds. When you're aloft in a plane and you gaze at the hillocks of cloud through which you are passing, underneath and above you, drifting: that's where the dead are, beyond their number and time (heaven is surely too crowded to believe in), constantly forming and reforming matter. Returning.

Dead. Death sentence.

But there's also such a thing as life sentence; going back again and again, no escape; this is infinity: reward, forgiveness, another chance or final punishment for all the misdeeds of all the karmas so far . . . only so far.

I understand.

It means you are condemned to live forever.

Notes

143   *. . . how few Westerners grasp malaria's devastation. . . .* 'Catch As Catch Can', *Los Angeles Times Book Review* (12/5/02), review by Dr Claire Panosian Dunavan of *The Fever Trail* by Mark Honigsbaum (Farrar, Straus and Giroux, 2002).

153   *. . . so man is continually peopling his current space with a world of his own.* A. P. Sinnett, *The Occult World* (Kessinger Publishing, 1981).

168   *Aorist: Denotes past action without indicating completion, continuation.* The American Heritage Dictionary of the English Language.

168   *Many times man lives and dies,*
       Between his two eternities
         That of race and that of soul.
   W. B. Yeats, 'Under Ben Bulben'.

175   *. . . sooner or later every action brings its retribution, in this existence or in one to come.* National Geographic (3/1/32), quoted by Ruth White, *Karma & Reincarnation* (Weiser Books, 2001).

193   *I have been part of it always and there is maybe no escape, forgetting and returning life after life like an insect in the grass.* W. B. Yeats.

203   *It turns out that something that never was and never will be is all that we have.* Amos Oz, *The Same Sea*, trans. Nicholas de Lange and the author (Harcourt, 1999).

211   *Just as everything is always something else . . . it may also throw some light on the procreative god.* Harry Mulisch, 'The Procedure,' trans. Paul Vincent (Viking, 2001).

214   *The Pestle of the moon*
          That pounds up all anew
          Brings me to birth again—
          To find what once I had,
          And know what once I have known.
      W. B. Yeats, 'On Woman.'

232   *The individual's choice of a future earthly body is limited, however.* . . .
      T. C. Lethbridge, *Witches* (Lyle Stuart, 1969), quoted by Ruth White,
      Karma & Reincarnation (Weiser Books, 2001).

236   *The doctrine of* karma *or* transmigration . . .' ibid.

DATE			